Gun Peril

Reed Bannerman expected trouble when he rode into Greasewood, for he had been summoned by the town marshal, Frank Neave, to take a job as deputy. But the situation was worse than he expected. Gold had been discovered in the nearby hills and its frightening influence affected everyone in town.

The explosive mixture of gold and jealousy was destined to give Bannerman the fight of his life. Now there was a murder to be solved and the wilfulness and machinations of just one man would put justice in doubt.

The thunder of guns rocked Greasewood and only Bannerman could restore peace – if he survived the final showdown.

Gun Peril

CORBA SUNMAN

A Black Horse Western

ROBERT HALE · LONDON

© Corba Sunman 2002
First published in Great Britain 2002

ISBN 0 7090 7107 8

Robert Hale Limited
Clerkenwell House
Clerkenwell Green
London EC1R 0HT

Typeset by
Derek Doyle & Associates, Liverpool.
Printed and bound in Great Britain by
Antony Rowe Limited, Wiltshire.

ONE

With a line of hills at his back, Reed Bannerman reined in on a knoll to take his first look at the town of Greasewood, Arizona. Easing himself in the hard saddle, he squinted his brown eyes against the glare of the overhead sun, hot and tired from a long ride, his hard muscles aching with fatigue. The brassy sun, in its high-noon position, cast very little shadow, and was torturous, baking the earth and everything upon it. He tilted his black Stetson forward over his eyes and subjected the distant town to an all-seeing scrutiny.

Apart from a turn-off on the left roughly one-third the way along, which led into the residential area of the town, there was just a single street stretching away from him in a shallow decline, arrow-straight until it bent a little to the right about halfway along, where it almost met a glinting creek. From there on it straightened out again, and seemed to stretch interminably towards the distant horizon as it inclined into the distance. He was surprised to see the place teeming with activity where he

5

had expected to find a sleepy cowtown. But he had heard that there was gold in the area, and the volume of traffic moving along the street proved the fact of the rumour.

An endless procession of heavily laden ore wagons, each pulled by a six-mule hitch, was emerging from a gash in the hills to Bannerman's right, following the trail to town like a line of ants. They passed along the main street, almost completely blocking the thorough-fare as they rolled forward ponderously heading for a cluster of stark buildings on the further side of the creek. A similar string of empty wagons was moving north from the buildings back to the workings in the hills, by-passing the town on the right. Bannerman could hear the distant monotonous pounding of heavy rock crushers processing the ore.

The sidewalks were crowded with townsfolk. He could even hear the noise that was emanating from that mass of humanity although he was still some way from the outskirts of the town. Three shots hammered as he studied the bustling scene, and he saw figures diving into cover as gun echoes faded sullenly. Then, like a colony of insects, the figures continued about their business as if shooting had never occurred.

Bannerman twisted in the saddle to look at his back trail and caught a glimpse of a little knot of people to his left, standing in a graveyard outside of town, heads bowed in respect for the occupant of a rough wooden coffin suspended over an oblong slash in the hard ground. An ornate hearse was being driven slowly away from the scene of the burial, heading back to town. At the foot of the grave, a minister, head bowed, was intent upon his Bible.

Tension seeped into Bannerman's chest as he rode towards the graveyard. He suspected that Greasewood had become a hell town, for its lawlessness was the reason for his arrival. He had been hired as a deputy marshal by Frank Neave, Greasewood's present town marshal. They had worked together for the law in Kansas a couple of years earlier. As Bannerman had realized when he received the urgent summons, Neave was likely to be in bad trouble here and needed another fast gun to back him.

A picket fence that was in need of repair surrounded the graveyard. Bannerman rode to the open gateway, dismounted, and tethered his sorrel to a rail near the entrance. There were a number of assorted vehicles – buggies and buckboards – parked along the edge of the cemetery. He eased the heavy cartridge belt buckled around his waist as he walked towards the silent group at the open grave, his right hand instinctively checking the big .45 Colt revolver holstered on his thigh. The chances were that Neave would be present at this ceremony, but his probing gaze, as he approached, did not pick out the lawman.

He paused in the background and looked around at the dozen or so assembled townsfolk, verifying that Neave was not present. The minister was reading the final prayers and, when he closed the Good Book, the undertaker and his helpers began to lower the coffin into its final resting place.

The mourners turned and began to disperse, most of them taking a covert look at the big, gun-hung stranger standing motionless at their rear. The last to leave was a tall, thin man wearing a deputy marshal badge on his green shirt, and Bannerman confronted him. The deputy halted and looked up enquiringly, his blue eyes narrowing as he took in the grim figure, his right hand dropping to the butt of his holstered gun.

'Howdy.' Bannerman's deep voice was pitched low. 'I'm looking for Frank Neave.'

The deputy's lips pulled tight. A sigh gusted from him, and his thin chest swelled as he drew a deep breath. He half turned towards the grave and jerked his chin in that direction. Making an attempt to speak, words failed him and he had to make a visible effort before he could operate his vocal chords.

'Frank's in that coffin. He was killed two nights ago.'

Bannerman froze in shock. He stood head and shoulders over the deputy, bulking large in his creased and dusty dark-blue store suit. His hard-boned face tightened into a grim mask as he digested the news, and his brown eyes took on a glint as he came to terms with it. For a moment his breathing stilled, then he forced his mind to combat the shock.

'Frank murdered!' He shook his head. 'Hell, I feel I've let him down. I'm Reed Bannerman. Frank sent for me a couple of weeks ago, saying he had a mite more trouble here than he could handle alone. I had some loose ends to tie up in Kansas or I would have got here sooner. Have you got the killer?'

The deputy shook his head. 'No one in town saw anything. Leastways, that's what folks who were on the street said. But these days, bad eyesight is common around Greasewood. I'm Joe Dack. Frank told me a whole lot about you, Bannerman. He was really looking forward to working with you again, and he got it fixed with the town council for you to step into the job the minute you showed up.' He paused, shaking his head sorrowfully. 'But everything's changed with Frank's death. And you may not want to take the job under these circumstances.'

'The least I'll want to do is find Frank's killer.' An ugly note sounded in Bannerman's voice. He exhaled slowly, his gaze fixed on the two men shovelling earth into the grave. 'And I'll need to wear a law badge while I'm hunting him.'

'Then we'd better go see Abe Thomas, the town mayor. He owns the lumber mill, and was saying only this morning that he'd be mighty relieved if you'll take on Frank's job. I'm fine as a deputy, but I wouldn't want the burden of being the town marshal. Things here have changed since gold was discovered in the hills. The town is bursting at the seams, and every thief and bad man in the country seem to have headed in this direction for easy pickings.'

Bannerman fell into step with Dack, and they walked to the edge of the graveyard, where Bannerman collected his horse and they continued to the town. Reaching town limits, Bannerman paused for a closer look at the bustling confusion along the street. A whip cracked close by and its lash struck the ground by his horse's right foot.

'Get the hell outa the road,' a harsh voice bellowed.

Bannerman turned swiftly, jerking his reins to move the sorrel to one side as a big ore wagon creaked and rumbled swayingly in the rutted tracks of the street. The driver, up on his high seat, glared down angrily and cracked his black-snake whip again as the heavy vehicle trundled by, pulled by six mules. The tip of the lash crackled ominously close to Bannerman's hat.

'That's one of the headaches you'll have around here.' Dack spoke in a clipped tone. 'Frank has tried to get EMC to by-pass the town, but Jake Moreny, the mining engineer, is a tough cuss who doesn't know the meaning of the word compromise. In fact, he takes great delight in the trouble he's causing by running the ore wagons right through the town.'

'Let's go talk to the mayor.' Bannerman spoke harshly. He waited for yet another ore wagon to rumble by, then followed closely, wrinkling his nose at the dust flying up from the churning wheels. He looked around keenly as they traversed the street, and, as they passed the front of a big saloon, two men emerged hurriedly through the batwings, wrestling and fighting furiously. They fell to the sidewalk, still grappling, before coming to a halt at Bannerman's feet.

One man tried to get to his feet while the second whipped out a knife from a sheath on his belt and swung his right hand in an attempt to stab his opponent. Bannerman stepped forward half a pace and kicked shrewdly with his right foot, connecting with the knifeman's wrist. Sunlight glinted on the naked blade as it flew through the air in a tight arc. The knifeman came lurching to his feet and reached for the butt of his holstered gun, his breathing laboured as he cursed Bannerman for interfering.

As the man grasped the butt of his gun, Bannerman palmed his Colt swiftly and crashed the long barrel against the man's left temple. Blood spurted and the man uttered a cry as he fell on his face in the thick dust. The other man stood motionless, shoulders heaving, gazing at Bannerman and Dack with obvious relief showing on his bruised, sweaty face.

'What was the fight about?' Bannerman demanded.

'The man on the ground is Ike Lazzard, chief trouble-shooter for EMC,' Dack volunteered. 'He's a bullying hardcase who has no respect for the law or anything else around here, except EMC. We've had a lot of problems with him and the other hardcases who call themselves trouble-shooters.'

'What is EMC?' Bannerman had already seen the initials on the ore wagons.

'Enterprise Mining Company.' Dack shook his head. 'I was kind of hoping you'd accept the town marshal's job before you came into contact with EMC.'

'So what was the fight about?' Bannerman repeated.

The man facing him shrugged heavy shoulders. 'Lazzard came looking for me,' he said wearily. 'My range meets the area where EMC are digging out the ore, and they want to take over some of my land. I'm Barney Todd.

I run the BT ranch west of town, and EMC reckon I'm too small to be of any account. They offered to buy me out – a real cheap deal – but I ain't selling for anything, so they are trying strong-arm tactics to make me quit. But, hell, I wouldn't sell the mineral rights to my property because EMC would ruin the place grubbing for their paydirt.'

'Sounds like EMC is a real rough-riding outfit.' Bannerman grimaced. 'OK, Todd, make yourself scarce, and try to stay out of Lazzard's way.' He looked into Dack's face. 'Are you gonna throw Lazzard in jail, or does he get away with disturbing the peace? What level of law-dealing did Frank set around here?'

'I reckon Frank was killed because he wouldn't let EMC get away with murder.' Dack grimaced. 'And if you're gonna take over as town marshal then you tell me what you want to do with Lazzard.'

'Jug him.' Bannerman picked up the knife discarded by Lazzard and handed it to Dack. He watched the big trouble-shooter, who was beginning to stir. 'I'll start as I mean to go on. Where's the jail?'

'A couple of blocks along the street from here.' Dack grinned. 'I was hoping you'd take a firm hand. But you better watch your step; EMC will put you down like they did Frank.'

'You reckon EMC is responsible for Frank's death?'

Dack shrugged his shoulders. 'There's bad trouble building up around here, and no one but EMC could be back of it. There was no trouble at all before gold was found in the hills. Greasewood was the most peaceful town in Creation.'

'Maybe.' Bannerman stirred the fallen man with the dusty toe of his boot. 'Come on, hard man. Are you gonna let a little tap on the head stop you? Get up and head for the calaboose. You look like you need to cool off, and you can rest up some in the town's free hotel while I consider what to charge you with.'

Lazzard lurched to his feet, uttering a string of curses. He faced up to Bannerman, a big, powerful man with arrogance in every muscle. He was at least six feet three inches tall and built as solidly as an ore wagon, with heavy arms and shoulders and a large head set on a bull-like neck. His blue eyes blazed with fury as he clenched his big hands into raw-boned clubs.

'You've just made the biggest mistake of your life, mister,' he rasped. 'I was going about my lawful business when you stuck your nose in. That'll cost you, and then some. Who in hell are you? I ain't seen you around before.'

'The way you're acting, you're gonna see a whole lot more of me in future,' Bannerman replied. 'And if you don't change your ways, pronto, I reckon you'll spend a lot of time inside the jail after I've pinned on the town marshal's badge.'

Lazzard's heavy face changed expression. His anger faded and wariness seeped into his gaze. 'So you're the hard man Frank Neave was talking about, huh?' He nodded. 'Mister, you better look at your cards real good before you start taking a hand in the game we're playing around here. Neave was warned several times to toe the line but he had no idea how to handle EMC.'

13

'Is that why he was murdered?' Bannerman tensed. 'If you know anything about Frank's death then spill it, Lazzard. It wouldn't be at all clever to clam up and force me to draw it from you.'

'Neave had plenty of chances to do what was right but he couldn't see past the badge he wore. Everything was black and white as far as he was concerned, and his attitude sure blocked progress.' Lazzard wiped blood from his face and shrugged his heavy shoulders. 'Give me my knife and gun and I'll get on about my business. But I'll be coming back to you later, mister, and when I do you better be wearing a different attitude.'

'Head for the jail,' Bannerman rasped. 'I'm putting you behind bars.'

'You're gonna jail me without a gun in your hand?' Lazzard began to grin. 'Hell, you've got a lot to learn about life in Greasewood. Why, the two of you together couldn't take me, even if I had one hand tied behind my back.'

His right fist suddenly swung in a swift, short arc, aimed at Bannerman's jaw, but it never reached its intended mark. Bannerman moved with the ease of long practice, taking Lazzard by surprise. The big trouble-shooter became unbalanced as his blow missed and, before he could recover, Bannerman's hard left fist lashed out with the speed of a striking rattler, his power aided by Lazzard's forward movement. The solid knuckles struck Lazzard's chin and stopped him in his tracks.

The impact was like an explosion. Lazzard was astonished. The blow seemed to paralyse the muscles of his neck and face. His head was jerked backwards and his feet began to move in the same direction as he tried to maintain his balance, for he was toppling over, his big figure already falling to the waiting dust of the street. A blackness slipped before his sight like a mask and his senses gyrated. A roaring sounded in his ears. He shook his head, but could not clear it of the effects of the blow.

Then another terrific punch smashed against the right side of his jaw and the blackness before his eyes was tattered by a myriad of stars cascading in scintillating colours through his tortured brain. It was a relief when full darkness imploded inside his head and he sprawled limply on the rutted ground.

Bannerman rubbed his knuckles, glancing around quickly, prepared for trouble if any of Lazzard's pards were nearby. He looked at Dack and saw admiration in the deputy's pale eyes.

'Frank sure didn't exaggerate when he said you could fight your weight in wildcats,' the deputy opined. 'You're gonna make a big difference to the local scene.'

'Help me throw Lazzard across my saddle,' Bannerman said. They grasped the man, heaved him up out of the dust, and settled him face-down across the saddle of the uneasy sorrel. Bannerman led the animal along the street, mindful that at least a score of townsmen had witnessed his victory and were following enthusiastically in the hope of seeing more action.

The town jail was built of adobe bricks, standing solid and four-square between Sutton's saloon and

Calder's Bank. Bannerman wrapped his reins around a tie rail in front of the jail and grasped Lazzard's chin lifting the man's head to check his condition. Lazzard's eyes were flickering, and Bannerman secured a grip on the man's gunbelt and hauled him out of the saddle to let him fall in a heap in the dust.

An ore wagon rumbled by at Bannerman's back, churning up dust which irritated his nostrils. He caught the sap-smell of newly milled lumber and saw a high-sided wagon pulling in at the sidewalk to his right. A short, fleshy, middle-aged man, whose face was more than half covered by a greying beard and long moustache, sprang down from the lumber wagon and came forward quickly, his expression changing swiftly as he recognized the big figure lying in the dust.

'Hell, that's Ike Lazzard,' he gasped. 'What happened to him? Was he run over by a wagon?'

'Heck no, Abe. It was something much worse.' Joe Dack chuckled hoarsely. 'This is Reed Bannerman, who we've been expecting to ride in. He taught Lazzard a lesson he'll never forget. Hit him with two punches, and Lazzard thought the sky had fallen in on him. Reed, this is Abe Thomas, the town mayor.'

'I'm sure glad to meet you, Bannerman.' Thomas stuck out a work-roughened hand. He looked diminutive beside Bannerman, the top of his head barely reaching Bannerman's broad shoulder. 'You've heard about Frank's murder, huh?'

'I heard,' Bannerman nodded.

''Are you ready to take over Frank's badge?' Thomas

16

reached into his vest pocket and produced a silver-coloured law star. He held it out on his open palm. 'I took it off Frank's shirt two nights ago. Had to wipe his blood off it. He'd been dead about five minutes when I got to him. It's yours for the asking. Frank told me a great deal about you, and he sure was looking forward to working with you again. But it wasn't to be, huh? I'll understand if you don't want to take the job now. Personally, I reckon the law department needs at least half-a-dozen deputies these days. I've been in touch with Sheriff Fenton, over in Rimrock, the county seat, and he's promised to send a deputy sheriff in here for a spell to relieve the situation.'

Bannerman looked at the badge and a bleak expression settled on his bronzed face as he reached out and took it, nodding slowly as he pinned it to his shirt. 'I'll wear it at least until I've picked up Frank's killer,' he said. 'But I'll need to be put straight on the local situation before I start operating.'

'Joe can give you the background to the trouble.' Thomas jumped towards the sidewalk as an ore wagon veered towards them. The driver was cursing a blue streak, cracking his heavy black-snake whip and directing the lash with uncanny accuracy at a woman who was driving a buggy the opposite way along the street. The lash struck the horse pulling the buggy and the animal lunged in a frenzied effort to escape, almost overturning the buggy. The woman cried out and dropped her reins as the vehicle lurched.

Bannerman sprang forward, leaping upwards for the

17

seat of the big ore wagon. He seized the driver's arm and snatched the whip from his grasp. The man cursed and swung a fist. Bannerman lowered his head a fraction and the blow missed. He jolted the man under the heart with his left fist and the driver collapsed with a groan and slumped on his seat. Bannerman grasped the man by the back of his belt, lifted him bodily, and dropped him over the side of the wagon into the dust of the street.

The woman in the buggy was calling to her fractious horse, trying to calm it. Bannerman noted that she was quite young, no more than twenty-five, and she was not being successful in her efforts to control the horse. He jumped down from the wagon, reached for the animal's reins, and quickly brought it under control.

'Thank you.' The girl's face was pale and set. 'This street is getting too bad to be true. When is something going to be done about these wagons coming through town? There's plenty of room out on the range for them. EMC is doing this deliberately to cause trouble.' She saw the marshal's star on Bannerman's shirt and lapsed into silence, then asked, 'Are you Frank Neave's friend from Kansas?'

He nodded. 'Reed Bannerman at your service, ma'am. I've stepped into Frank's boots, and I plan to do something about the town as soon as I get the lowdown on what's happening around here.'

'I'm Ellen Calder, Mr Bannerman. My father is Brent Calder, the banker.' She was poised, possessing an inner serenity that struck a chord in Bannerman's chest. Her oval-shaped face was framed by golden curls, and he found her good to look upon. There was strength of character in her countenance, but there was a coldness in her blue eyes that seemed at odds with her appearance. 'I'd be happy to have you call for supper this evening, Mr Bannerman. Our house is the last one on the right going along the residential road.'

'Thank you, Miss Calder.' He smiled. 'I'd like to take you up on your offer. I'll call about eight o'clock, if my duties don't prevent me.'

'What's the hold up here?' a harsh voice cut in, and a big man wearing twin guns on the crossed cartridge belts around his waist came thrusting through the crowd that had gathered around the ore wagon and buggy. He saw the driver on the ground and bent over the man, pulling him face upwards. 'What happened?' he demanded, his hands dropping to his gun butts. 'Who put this guy to sleep?'

'I did,' Bannerman said quietly.

The hardcase looked him up and down, his critical gaze taking in the star on Bannerman's shirt. Then he half lifted his right-hand pistol from its holster. Bannerman thought he was going to complete the draw and flashed into action, drawing his gun and cocking it in a movement that was too swift for eyes to follow. The hardcase was still gripping his gun butt, and his mouth gaped when he found himself looking into the barrel of Bannerman's pistol.

'Hold up there,' he gasped. 'I wasn't about to pull my gun. We got a tight schedule to meet with these ore wagons and I need to get this one rolling again or there'll be a big tail-back. I'll report this incident to Ike Lazzard. He's EMC's top gun, and he'll deal with you.'

'If you want to talk to Lazzard you better do it before I throw him in jail, ' Bannerman responded. He jerked a thumb in the direction of the groggy trouble-shooter, who was now sitting on the edge of the sidewalk with his head in his hands.

'Jeez!' The hardcase shook his head in amazement. 'There'll be hell to pay over this. Just wait till Moreny hears about it. He'll ride in here with a dozen men and stomp you into the dust, badge and all. He'll eat you, guts and feathers.'

'Get out of here, and when you see Moreny, tell him I'll be looking him up pretty soon. He's gonna have to learn what he can and cannot do around town. Killing the town marshal was one helluva bad move by whoever did it, and it'll get even worse around here for trouble-makers now I'm wearing the law badge.'

The trouble-shooter backed away, then turned and pushed back through the assembled crowd. Bannerman holstered his gun with a slick movement. He had spelled it out plain and simple, but realized that it would take more than mere words to subdue the trouble presently crowding Greasewood.

TWO

'If that's a sample of the way you work then you're gonna be fine around here,' Abe Thomas said excitedly. 'Frank sure didn't lie when he said you're one of the best. But it's a pity you didn't get here sooner, Bannerman; Frank might still be alive if you had.'

Bannerman nodded, his dark gaze watching Ellen Calder as she drove her buggy on along the street. His pulses seemed to race. Usually he was insensitive to women, but Ellen Calder had stirred him, although he had sensed that she was overburdened with some kind of trouble. He stifled his emotion and grasped Ike Lazzard's collar, shaking the big man to full consciousness.

'Let's put this one behind bars,' he said curtly.

'What about the driver of that wagon?' Dack demanded.

The man in question was stirring, pushing himself up to his hands and knees and shaking his head experimentally. He regained his feet, staggered, and had to lean against the side of his big wagon while recovering

21

his equilibrium. The driver of the wagon behind came kicking through the thick dust towards them, enquiry showing on his bearded face. He was carrying a Winchester in his right hand.

'What the hell is goin' on?' he demanded. 'We got to keep 'em rolling. What happened to you, Benson?'

'I happened to him,' Bannerman rasped. 'And I'll tell you what to do: go back to town limits and warn all drivers to stay out of the street. As of this minute, no wagons are to pass through town.'

'You must be crazy if you figure you can stop us,' the man blustered. 'Wait till Lazzard hears about this. He'll stop your wind in two seconds.'

'Tell him about it now.' Bannerman stepped aside to reveal his prisoner to the driver's shocked gaze. Lazzard was slumped on the edge of the sidewalk, face bloodied and pale, his eyes showing distress. 'But I guess he ain't caring about his job right now. And unless you want to join him in jail then you'll do like I said: stop the wagons from entering the street. They are banned from town limits.'

The driver shook his head, uncertainty showing in his weathered features. But he made no attempt to resist, despite the rifle in his hand. He turned and went back the way he had come. Bannerman could see three other wagons stopped in the rear, completely blocking the north end of the street. Dozens of townsfolk were converging on the spot, and there was a hubbub of excited talk as they awaited developments.

'We're right behind you in this,' Thomas said. 'We

22

don't want these wagons, in the street day and night. But EMC are tough, and we've not had anyone strong enough to stop them.'

'Can you handle Lazzard, Joe?' Bannerman demanded.

Dack drew his pistol and cocked it. 'Consider him handled.' He grinned. 'You knocked the starch out of him. I'll put him behind bars with no trouble, and come back to handle anyone else you want jugged.'

Bannerman went to the driver he had downed and grasped his shoulder. Exerting his strength, he thrust the man up into his high seat on the ore wagon.

'Get moving. You can travel the street this last time. But after this stay out of town limits, and that goes for all the wagons. Tell your boss what I say, and don't get in my way in future. I'll sure remember your face, mister.'

The man picked up his discarded whip and cracked it, setting his six-mule hitch into motion. The vehicle swayed along the street towards the turn-off to the smelter and Bannerman watched for a moment, then swung into his saddle and rode back to the wagon next in line. The driver had resumed his seat and sat gazing sullenly at him. Repeating his instructions, Bannerman continued back along the line of wagons, issuing the same order until he reached the outskirts of town. The wagons were tailing back along the trail now, and he rode in to confront the driver of the wagon that was waiting to enter the street.

'What's holding us up?' the man demanded. 'We got a tight schedule. Where's Lazzard? He should be sorting this out.'

'Pull off to the right and make your way to the factory across those back lots,' Bannerman rasped.

'The hell you say! I can't do that.' The driver shook his head. 'Lazzard would have my guts.'

'I'll throw you in jail if you don't,' Bannerman snapped. 'Get moving. The rest of the wagons will follow the same route. And none of you will come through town again. Now jump to it or I'll arrest you for loitering.'

The driver remained motionless, digesting the news. Then he shook his head. 'I can't do that without Lazzard's say-so,' he protested. 'It's more than my job is worth. Who in hell are you, anyway? Where did you come from?'

'It doesn't matter who I am. I'm running the local law now, and you'll do like you're told. Lazzard is in jail, and you'll join him there if you don't move out now.' Bannerman dropped his right hand to the butt of his gun.

The driver shook his head and took up his reins. He got his mules pulling together and the wagon swung off the trail to the right, heading away from the street and raising banners of grey dust across the back lots. Bannerman sat his horse in the middle of the trail, signalling to the rest of the wagons to follow the leader, and when the first six vehicles were moving steadily away from the street he wiped sweat from his forehead and rode back into town, where the last ore wagon there was moving forward, leaving the street clear for the first time in months.

Abe Thomas was sitting on his wagon, his face a study in disbelief, looking around the street. A great crowd of townsfolk blocked the sidewalks on either side. The whole town had come to a standstill, and silence lay heavily upon it. Bannerman realized that everyone was waiting for the next incident to develop, and swung out of his saddle to wrap his reins around a convenient rail. He saw two riders coming fast along the street from the direction of the smelter. They looked like trouble-shooters, and he rested his hand on the butt of his holstered gun as he waited for them to arrive.

The two riders had all the earmarks of hardcases. Both were heavily armed and apparently filled with deadly intent. They reined up a couple of feet in front of Bannerman and looked him over.

'Are you the galoot who stopped the wagons coming through here?' one of them demanded.

'Yeah. And they won't use the street again. I've set them by-passing the town, and they better stick to that or there'll be real trouble.'

'Mister, you don't know what you're getting into.' The smaller of the two riders swung out of his saddle and confronted Bannerman. 'I draw pay to keep things smooth for EMC, and you're riling me considerable. I don't need this kind of hassle. My orders are clear: stop anyone trying to give us trouble. You're wearing a gun so turn your hand loose. You got five seconds before I make my move.'

Bannerman did not move a muscle. He waited out the interminable seconds. His right hand was down at his side, the inside of his wrist lightly touching the butt of his holstered gun. The silence around him was intense. He breathed lightly, watching the gunman. The man started his play without warning. His right hand lifted and grasped the butt of his holstered weapon, and the gun seemed to leap into his hand with a movement almost too swift to follow.

Bannerman whipped into action, triggered by the changing expression in the man's eyes a split second before he started to draw, and his own gun was in his hand before the gunman's Colt cleared leather. He thumbed back his hammer before the weapon had levelled, and the crash of his shot sent a wave of shock through the watching crowd. His gun smoked and bucked as the speeding bullet took the gunman in the right shoulder, stopping his draw and sending him on to his back in the thick dust.

Bannerman cocked his gun and pointed the weapon at the second rider, who was reaching for his gun. The man paused, his weapon half-drawn, and for an interminable moment he stared death in the face. Then he thrust the weapon deep into its holster and lifted his hands away from his body, palms outwards.

'I don't want no part of this,' he said loudly.

'You left it mighty late, but get rid of your gun and then ride out of here.' Bannerman spoke firmly. 'Report to your boss. Tell him what's happened in town, and warn him that no more wagons are to use the street.'

The man took his gun from his holster, using forefinger and thumb only, and dropped the weapon into the dust before wheeling his mount and riding back the way he had come. Bannerman holstered his weapon with a slick movement and looked around, his dark eyes slitted and filled with deadly intent.

'Someone better fetch the doc,' he suggested. He raised his voice, and sent echoes around the street as he advised the townsfolk to go about their business. Abe Thomas chucked his reins and sent his team along the street, a wide grin on his face. He lifted a hand to Bannerman as he departed.

'I hope you can make this stick,' he called. 'I like the town this way. But you better pick out a couple more deputies. Some men around here have been getting away with murder. And watch your back. Don't forget that Frank was gunned down from behind only a couple of nights ago.'

'That's something I won't forget,' Bannerman replied. He swung into his saddle and sat the animal, using the extra height to check out the now almost deserted street. He looked around intently, able to see the line of ore wagons coming along the trail to town and turning off before reaching the street. He had won the first round, but was experienced enough in such matters to be aware that the conclusion might turn out quite differently.

Joe Dack marched Lazzard into the jail and Bannerman dismounted and followed. It was slightly cooler inside the office. Dack put Lazzard behind bars with a great deal of clattering of metal doors, and

27

emerged from the cell block with a wide grin on his expressive face.

'Joe, have you got any ideas for a couple of extra deputies?' Bannerman asked.

Dack grimaced and shook his head. 'There are half-a-dozen men around town who would be great at backing us, but Frank discovered when he tried to enlist them, that nobody is keen to become a target. The odds are too great. Men will wait and watch to see how you get on before taking any chances and, even if you look like pulling it off, they may still hang back.'

'I can't say that I blame them.' Bannerman walked to the open door and glanced out at the quiet street.

Dack joined him and looked around. A shadow crossed his face. 'This is the lull before the storm,' he observed. 'Right now Jake Moreny will be getting the news of what you've done here, and he ain't a man to sit on the fence. He'll come riding in with a handful of his trouble-shooters and we'll be treated to a dose of gun music, compliments of EMC.'

'Where does Moreny hang out?' Bannerman slid his pistol out of its holster and reloaded the spent chamber. 'I'll pay him a visit. He sounds like the type who can't accept the inevitable so I'd better drop in on him and spell it out.'

'He's got an office out by the factory. But you can't go in there alone: you'd never come out alive. Frank is dead because he didn't accept Moreny for what he is.'

'Have you got any evidence concerning Frank's death? Any pointers at all?'

Dack shook his head. 'I'm afraid there's nothing. But I guess we all know that EMC is back of it.'

'Knowing ain't good enough. We work on proof. Was Frank threatened at all during his last days? You would have been closest to him during that time. I need to get things straight in my mind; even the smallest incident might be important. Fill me in on the background.'

'Frank always had trouble with EMC's trouble shooters, who were acting on orders. Lazzard leads that bunch but he gets his instructions from Moreny.'

'So I'll go talk to Moreny. ' Bannerman went to the sorrel and swung into his saddle. He grinned but there was a grim expression on his angular face. 'See you when I get back.'

'Hey, I better go with you,' Dack said quickly. 'They're shooting lawmen around here.'

'You keep an eye on the street,' Bannerman insisted. 'I can handle this.'

He rode along the street towards the creek, moving at a canter, his keen eyes taking in details of the buildings on either side of the deeply rutted thoroughfare. There seemed to be a preponderance of saloons and gaming places which told him a great deal about the way the town had grown.

A cut-off had been made between the livery barn and a store, and tracks showed Bannerman the way the ore wagons had left the street to make for the smelter. He followed, skirting the factory buildings, making for a cabin that stood alone on the right of the trail. He squinted his eyes against the sun and looked along the back lots of the buildings fronting the street, nodding when he saw the two lines of wagons; one, heavily laden with ore, heading towards the smelter, and the other, empty, returning to the hills in the opposite direction. The whole business was proceeding smoothly, and he realized just how big the Enterprise Mining Company's operation really was.

He dismounted at the door of the cabin and wrapped his reins around the tie rail outside. The door opened as he turned to face the squat building and a big, gun-hung man emerged, his right hand resting on the butt of his holstered pistol. There was truculence etched into the man's expression, and it deepened when he saw the star pinned to Bannerman's shirt front.

'You ain't welcome here,' he snarled. 'Get back on that nag and beat it.'

'I want to see Jake Moreny. Is he here?'

'If he sees you it'll be through gunsmoke. Get outa here or I'll run you out.'

Bannerman smiled easily, but a flame had ignited in his heart and he clenched his big hands convulsively as he clung to a corner of his self-control. He was getting tired of the general attitude presented by EMC's trouble-shooters. 'I'd like to see you try to run me out, using fists, guns, or anything else you might have in mind,' he challenged.

His quietly spoken words took the bluster out of the hardcase. The man gripped the butt of his gun, but something in Bannerman's manner held him back.

'Either pull it or get your hand away from it,' Bannerman rasped.

Before the man could decide, the door of the cabin was jerked open and a big, fleshy man stepped into the doorway. He was a tight-lipped, big-nosed individual whose burly figure was strong and solid. Thrusting his left shoulder against a doorpost, he leaned his considerable weight against it, causing the sun-baked wood to creak in protest. There was arrogance in every line of his heavy body. He looked what he was, a man accustomed to being obeyed instantly in everything, and there was the unbridled gleam of a wild bull in his brown eyes that bespoke of an unchained temper.

'Jake Moreny?' Bannerman demanded.

Moreny ignored him, his attention on the trouble-shooter. 'What's your problem, Comer?' he demanded, in a gravelly voice. 'I hire you to keep bums outa here but this galoot is facing you down. You're fired if you can't handle your chores.'

The hardcase drew a deep breath, but evidently figured that the situation was out of his control. 'He's the new town marshal, Jake,' he rasped. 'Looks like he's here on town business. I can't just gun him down.'

'Why not?' Bannerman demanded. 'Ain't that what happened to Frank Neave?'

'All right, Comer.' Moreny straightened from his indolent position. 'Get out and leave this to me. Go find Lazzard. The big punk is never around when I want him. Look in the saloons, and if you find him in one then tell him to fork his bronc outa here for other

31

parts, because he'll be through in this job.'

There was relief in Comer's expression as he departed. Bannerman did not relax his vigilance. He half-turned to watch the man's departure whilst keeping an eye on Moreny. The big mining engineer chuckled, but there was no amusement in his tone.

'I was about to come into the street to check on you, mister,' he rasped. 'What's the big idea, turning my wagons away from the route I picked for them?'

'What was your idea sending them along the street and blocking it when it was just as easy for them to follow their present route?' Bannerman kept his tone neutral. 'I figure it to be in your best interests to rub along easy with the town instead of raising hell. You look like a man who plays the percentages in any situation, so why cause unnecessary trouble?'

Moreny straightened in the doorway, his right hand resting on the butt of the gun holstered on his right hip. For a moment, Bannerman figured there would be gun-play but did not change his own posture. His gunhand was down at his side.

'If you reckon to use your gun then get to it,' he said crisply. 'But if that thought ain't in your mind then keep your hand well clear of the weapon.'

'What's on your mind?' Moreny let his gunhand drop to his side. 'I'm the feller that runs this whole business, and I ain't got no time to jaw. I can't think of anything you could have to do with me, so climb back on your nag and hoof it out of here. Time-wasters ain't welcome.'

Bannerman's dark gaze hardened but he smiled. 'Spare me the tough stuff, Moreny. I cut my eye teeth on guys like you. Let's clear the air so we can get down to the real business. If you fancy your chances then go ahead and pull your gun. But if you do, I'll kill you. Or you can try your fists. I'm easy either way. I'm here to lay down the law to you and make it stick, and I know I can't do it while you hold your present attitude. Apart from that, I don't like your manner. You need to be taught respect, so make up your mind now. What's it to be? Guns or fists? It's that, or you'll pull in your horns and rub along easy with the town. Now's the time to make up your mind. We can settle all the trouble here and now.'

Moreny blinked, shaken by Bannerman's cold-bloodedness. He shrugged his massive shoulders, his dark eyes brooding. Then he heaved a long sigh and shook his head.

'Where did you get the idea from that I'm against the law?' he rasped. 'I have a tough job to do and I handle it the best way I can. I have to work against the clock. I can't trust half the men working for me, and I never got any help from the local law.'

'You set yourself up against the law,' Bannerman insisted. 'The way you had those ore wagons rolling along the street, it was a slap in the face for every law-abiding man in town. I'm tempted to jug you for thumbing your nose at the law, and if you don't pull in your horns real quick you will see the inside of the jail.'

'Come into the office for a drink,' Moreny offered. '

I don't have much time to spare, but if I got to make a peace overture then let's get it done.'

'You don't have to convince me of anything.' Bannerman did not relax his guard. 'I'll judge you on your actions, and if you overstep the mark anywhere along the line then I'll come for you. No more ore wagons through the town. And keep a tight rein on your so-called trouble-shooters. If they break the law they'll go into the jail.'

'The miners working for EMC are a tough bunch.' Moreny grimaced. 'They work and play hard, and what they do when they're not grubbing for paydirt is none of my business. It's your job to keep them in line.'

'I'm not talking about the miners. I'll handle them. You keep your hardcases in line, or pretty soon you won't have any.'

'That's big talk.' Moreny grinned, but there was an ugly expression in his blue eyes. 'You figure you're that good with a gun, huh? Well, I got some pretty fast hands in my crew.'

Bannerman realized that he would get no further with the mining boss. But he had issued his warning and was satisfied. He swung into his saddle, turning the sorrel so that Moreny was in front of him all the time. Moreny shrugged and turned abruptly to enter the office. He slammed the door with a force that shook the door frame, and Bannerman smiled as he rode back into town. He had the feeling that, for all his bluster, Moreny knew when he was beaten. But he would always be very dangerous.

He turned into the livery barn when he reached the street, putting the sorrel at the water trough to let it drink its fill. The liveryman appeared as he led the animal into a stall; an old man who looked about eighty and limped badly, favouring his left side. The oldster brought a scoop of oats and dumped it into the manger, then fetched a forkful of sweet-smelling hay, which he put into a rack on the wall just above the sorrel's head.

'So you're the new marshal, huh?' he commented, leaning on his pitchfork outside the stall while Bannerman attended to his horse. 'I'm Rafe Dunne. I own the stable. You'll have to be extra good to fill Frank Neave's boots; he was a lawman and a half!'

'And he was killed two nights ago.' Bannerman removed his saddle-bags from the cantle and slung them over a rail. He unsaddled and placed the heavy leather gear over a rack. Taking his Winchester from its boot, he hefted it in his right hand and picked up his saddle-bags. 'Can you tell me anything about Frank's murder?' He looked directly into the ostler's pale eyes as he asked the question, and saw fear and doubt in them. The old man backed off a couple of paces.

'I don't know a blame thing,' he said, 'and if I did I wouldn't talk. It ain't safe just to step out on to the street these days. There's always someone around ready to steal your money or bully you. And don't think you'll be able to make a difference to the set-up. They'll put you under just like they did poor Frank. I never knew a better man that the town marshal, and I attended his funeral today.'

Bannerman started for the wide doorway, saddle-bags over his left shoulder and his Winchester in his left hand. He was stepping out into the sunlight in front of the stable when a voice hailed him from the rear door of the big barn.

'Hey, Marshal. This way.'

Bannerman moved instinctively, hurling himself to the left and scrambling around as he hit the straw-covered ground on his left shoulder. His right hand snaked his pistol out of its holster and he cocked the weapon as he peered around for the owner of the voice. A gun blasted from the shadows just inside and to the right of the open rear door and the bullet struck the ground an inch from Bannerman's left elbow as he trig-gered a response, aiming at the gun flash that speared out of the gloom. He bracketed the area with three shots, then changed his position fast, his ears half deaf-ened by the gun thunder racketing across the town....

THREE

Bannerman rolled over and came up into the aim again, his gun muzzle weaving slightly as he looked for his attacker. He restrained his breathing. Pungent gunsmoke was rasping his throat. His nerves were taut, his reflexes hair-triggered. He saw movement in the patch of gloom where he had directed his first shots, but held his fire when a figure staggered forward a couple of uneasy steps, smoking gun spilling from its hand. The man pitched forward on to his face like a falling tree and lay inert.

Bannerman got to his feet, gun ready. The ostler was in a state of frozen shock, clutching his pitchfork as if his life depended on it. Bannerman passed the old man and walked towards the motionless figure. He could see the man's discarded gun lying in the straw just beyond reach of an outflung hand. There was blood on the man's shirt front and on his face, and Bannerman did not need a second glance to see that he was dead.

He kicked the gun clear of the dead hand and

looked into the man's face, recognizing the trouble-shooter who had approached him on the street after Lazzard had been arrested. A voice spoke from the front of the barn and he turned quickly, gun lifting like a snake scenting prey. He relaxed when he saw Dack standing in the front doorway, shoulders heaving breathlessly from running.

'I figured they'd got you when I heard the shooting.' Dack came forward to peer down at the dead man. He grimaced. 'That's Pete Ellis, one of EMC's trouble-shooters. I wondered how long it would take those hardcases to start making a play for you.'

'About how many of them are there?' Bannerman demanded. 'If they're gonna be this troublesome then we'd better round them up and jug them.'

'I doubt if the jail would be big enough to house them all. ' Dack shook his head. 'And Moreny has only to snap his fingers to have another dozen or so at his beck and call.'

'Then we'll make Moreny responsible for the behaviour of his crew, and arrest him if they step out of line. I guess there's an undertaker in town, huh? Get him to handle the body. I'm gonna get me some food, then I'll go back to see Moreny.'

'You've seen him already?' Dack sounded surprised.

Bannerman smiled grimly. 'He ain't so tough. I told him a few things. But we're gonna have to wait for his reaction.'

'Ellis wouldn't have come at you without orders.'

'We'll wait and see.' Bannerman picked up his rifle

38

and saddle-bags. As he walked to the front doorway he saw half-a-dozen men standing outside in the background, peering into the gloom inside the building. 'Any of Moreny's men out there?' he demanded.

'None that I can see.' Dack checked quickly. 'That guy in the black suit is Bill Naylor, the undertaker. He's usually first on the scene after a shooting. He's sure got a nose for business, and it looks like you're gonna give him a good living.'

Bannerman walked out of the barn into the sunlight and looked around. 'Where's the nearest eating-house?' he demanded.

'Ma Lambert's place is up there on the left. Best food in town. What are you gonna do about sleeping?'

'I'll sleep on the job. There'll always be a spare bed in the jail. I'll need to be on hand, at least until I settle in. See you at the jail in about thirty minutes.'

Dack nodded and went to where the undertaker was standing. Bannerman walked on along the sidewalk, his vigilance keen, his thoughts working remotely. Killing Ellis had not affected him for he had become accustomed to the presence of death, which had accompanied his way of life for a number of years. He had upheld the law in several tough towns, gaining a reputation that was second to none. In the name of his law-dealing he had seen men killed and had prevented men from killing each other. The gun holstered on his hip had blasted fourteen men to hell and gone. He was at the top of his grim profession, capable of fighting the lawlessness that flourished here in Greasewood, but apart from all that, he was keenly aware that he needed luck on his side.

Ma Lambert's restaurant was a large room with small tables clustered between the door and the rear counter. Bannerman paused in the doorway and looked around. The place, almost empty now, was very clean. There were white cloths on the tables. A waitress, smartly attired in a blue dress and starched apron, with a neat blue bow in her hair, was attending to the needs of the few remaining diners scattered around the room. There was a welcoming aroma of well-cooked, good, wholesome food pervading the place. The waitress spotted Bannerman's entrance and came towards him, smiling a welcome. She hesitated at the sight of the star on his shirt front, then came forward again, the smile on her pretty face now somewhat strained. Bannerman noted her change of expression and was intrigued by it.

'Do you require a meal or just coffee, sir?' she asked in a pleasant tone.

'A meal,' he responded. 'I haven't eaten since before sun-up this morning. I'll have whatever's going, and make it a big portion. If I like the food I'll be eating here every day for as long as I hold down this job. Mebbe you can tell me the best time to drop in on you. I prefer to feed when the rush has finished.'

'Certainly. This is about the best time to miss the rush.' She glanced at his badge. 'And you're the new town marshal.' She pointed towards an empty table in a corner where he would be able to watch the door and the rest of the room. 'Frank Neave used to eat here.'

Her tone faltered slightly, and Bannerman frowned as he detected it. She swallowed as if she had a lump in her throat. 'I heard that you were a close friend of Frank.'

'As close as a man can get,' Bannerman nodded. 'We worked together for the law in Kansas. Frank saved my life on more than one occasion, and I was able to do the same for him. It's a pity I didn't get here before he was killed: I might have prevented his death.'

'I'm June Tate.' She spoke quietly, her blue eyes dull with suppressed grief. 'Frank and I had an understanding. We were very good friends.' She turned away quickly and hurried into the kitchen.

Bannerman clenched his teeth as an unaccustomed wave of emotion surged through him. He dumped his saddle-bags on a nearby chair and propped his Winchester against the wall at his side as he sat down, heaving a long sigh. He could guess that Frank's death had left a big hole in this community. He drew his gun and checked the weapon, then slid it back into its holster. With any luck he would see Frank's killer through gunsmoke before too long.

His attention was attracted to three men who were seated at a window table across the big room. They were talking loudly, and one was watching Bannerman without making his action too obvious, looking away quickly when Bannerman glanced at him. Bannerman stiffened imperceptibly as he ran his gaze over the trio. Hardcases! It was written all over them, in appearance and manner. He tensed, mentally preparing himself for

41

possible action. They seemed to be the kind of men who would give him trouble.

The man watching him was powerfully built, tall and square-featured. He had a lantern jaw, and the long bones of his face were angular under the weathered skin stretched tautly across his cadaverous cheeks. The prominent bulge of his chin was softened by black whiskers, but, despite the cover, his lower face looked out of proportion to the rest of his features. He had narrowed brown eyes which were gleaming with an unholy light, and when he spoke his tone was flat and nasal.

Bannerman watched the trio without making it obvious. The second man was dark-skinned, almost copper-coloured, and massively built, a huge man with well-developed shoulders and arms that over-stretched the thin fabric of his red shirt to the point of splitting it. His moon face showed signs of many beatings around the eyes, his cheeks puffy and ravaged by scar tissue. His voice rasped like an old barn door, and he spoke in a harsh, low tone.

June Tate interrupted Bannerman by placing a food-filled plate before him. He thanked her and began eating, intent on filling his empty stomach while the opportunity presented itself. He had the feeling that when he really settled into his job, quiet moments like this would be few and far between. But the waitress did not move away, and he glanced up at her.

'Something wrong?' he queried.

'I feel I ought to warn you about those three men sitting at the window seat across the room.' She spoke quietly, hesitantly, a tinge of worry in her voice. 'They have eaten, and while I was serving them I heard scraps of their conversation. They didn't seem to care who overheard them, and I suspect, from what was said, that they're up to no good.'

'Have they been in town long?' He glanced past her slender figure to study the trio he had been watching. The third man was short and fat with a permanent scowl on his fleshy face. His Stetson was pushed back off his forehead to reveal a mass of red hair. His watery blue eyes were furtive, shooting quick glances around to take stock of his surroundings.

'Two days, I think,' she said.

'What was said to arouse your suspicions?' Bannerman forked food into his mouth to get through the meal in case trouble should break out.

'The big man with the long chin and beard seems to be their leader. They call him Hack. He was talking about the bank, said there should be a fortune in it. The man with the massive shoulders is Mick. He's got a very harsh voice. I heard him say something about the local law. You'd better be on your guard, Marshal.'

'Thanks for the warning. I had pegged them as likely trouble-makers.' Bannerman did not pause in his eating. 'Have they been here before?'

'They came in for food about two o'clock yesterday afternoon. That was the first time I saw them. There was another with them then. He's little more than a boy, aged about seventeen, I should think. He seemed over-anxious about something – nervous of his own shadow.

I remember wondering what he was doing with such hardcases. I haven't seen him since yesterday. He hasn't been in at all today.'

Bannerman nodded. 'Don't worry about it. I'll keep my eyes skinned, and I'll check them out later. But thanks for the warning.'

The street door was opened as she nodded and turned to depart. Bannerman glanced around and saw that the newcomer was a tall, powerfully built young man dressed in expensive range clothes. Something in the man's manner alerted Bannerman, and he noted belligerence in the man's scowling expression.

'June,' he called, 'what the hell have you been doing? You've kept me waiting. When I tell you to come over to the hotel at a certain time I expect you to do it. Get rid of that apron and come with me.'

The girl's face reddened as her eyes filled with anger. She glanced at Bannerman, who was eating stolidly, before facing the arrogant newcomer.

'I don't take orders from you, Pete Morell,' she snapped. 'And how many times do I have to tell you to stay away from me? If Frank was alive he'd beat your ears off for chasing after me.' She laughed mirthlessly. 'But then, you wouldn't have stepped out of line if Frank hadn't been murdered.'

Morell came towards Bannerman's table, his spurs tinkling musically. He reached out and grasped the girl's left wrist, and she exclaimed in pain as she tried to wrench free. Bannerman dropped his fork and clamped his strong fingers around the man's wrist, exerting his strength, and the cowboy cursed in pain, releasing the girl. Bannerman gained his feet, still holding the man's wrist.

'You're annoying the lady,' he said crisply. 'Get out of here before you go too far.'

'Who in hell are you?' Morell demanded, trying to break Bannerman's grip on his wrist. He changed his tactics suddenly and reached for his holstered gun. Bannerman instantly sledged up his right fist and connected with the man's jaw.

Morell went over backwards, out cold, and Reed Bannerman released his hold on the wrist and let the man fall to the floor. The three men at the window table started up nervously, but sat down again when they saw the badge on Bannerman's shirt. Bannerman bent and took the gun from Morell's holster.

'So he's been giving you trouble since Frank was killed, huh?' he demanded, placing the pistol on the table and sitting to resume his meal. 'Well he won't bother you again. Go about your business. I'll wise him up when he comes round.'

'Thank you.' She spoke quietly, rubbing her wrist. 'He has been making a nuisance of himself.' She departed and, as she returned to the kitchen, the big man at the window table signalled to her. Bannerman heard him asking tersely for their bill.

'I'll pay for another dinner,' Bannerman overheard him say. 'There's a young feller with us who'll be in to eat shortly. He's busy right now. But he'll sure be hungry. Make certain he gets enough to eat, will you?'

'I know who you mean,' the waitress responded. 'I saw him with you yesterday. I'll feed him well.'

Bannerman had finished his meal by the time the three men arose from the table and departed, all casting curious glances at him and the now stirring cowboy lying on the floor. He was drinking coffee when Morell began to rise, and paused to study the youngster.

Morell was about twenty-three, well set up, with brown eyes and black wavy hair. He swayed when he stood erect, and felt for his gun to find the holster empty. The gun lay beside Bannerman's plate and he eyed it longingly, the fingers of his gunhand crooking as he fought against the impulse to reach for it.

'Sit down opposite me,' Bannerman suggested, finishing his coffee. 'In case you haven't grasped the fact yet, I'm the new town marshal, and I don't like men who bully women. You work for one of the local ranches, huh?'

'My pa owns Circle M.' Morell sat down heavily.

'You better pull in your horns after this.' Bannerman laid his hand on the gun on the table. 'Now get outa here. You can pick up your gun from the law office when you've had a chance to cool off. Go on, beat it, and try to remember that I won't stand any nonsense from anyone around here, no matter who he is. You got that?'

Morell stared at him for a moment or so. He seemed about to disobey, then moistened his thin lips and got to his feet to depart without comment. Bannerman looked up when the street door opened within seconds of Morell's departure, thinking the man was returning, but a youngster of about seventeen entered to pause uncertainly in the doorway. Bannerman's keen gaze took in his appearance. The thing about the youth that struck Bannerman forcibly was the youngster's chin, which resembled that of the man called Hack. It was prominent, to say the least, and seemed to be a family trait. The youth's face was young-looking, and wore a serious expression. He seemed self-conscious, awkward, and came towards a vacant table near to Bannerman. At the last moment he looked at Bannerman, and his eyes widened when he spotted the star on Bannerman's chest, which caused him to shy away like a startled foal. He blundered towards a table across the room, knocking over a chair in his haste.

Bannerman watched him indifferently and saw him pick up the chair. His face had reddened and he sank thankfully into a seat at the table recently vacated by his three tough companions. The waitress approached him, reasssured him, and he nodded vehemently in reply to her question. She hurried into the kitchen to return moments later with a large plate filled with food. Bannerman was looking elsewhere when the youngster subjected him to one of numerous glances, but he missed nothing of the youngster's manner.

Bannerman wondered why such a green-looking youth was siding three tough hardcases. He finished his coffee and lifted a finger to the waitress. Paying the bill, he arose, and looked down at her face from his greater height.

'Thank you, ' he said loudly enough for the youth to hear. 'I haven't tasted such good food in a long time. I'll make a point of eating here in future.' He paused and then lowered his voice. 'Don't worry about Morell. I'll have another talk with him when he comes to the law office to pick up his gun.'

'I hope you won't have any trouble from the Circle M outfit. Pete Morell has two or three tough cowboys who loaf around with him, and they do anything he orders. I wish he hadn't come in at that moment.'

'He's probably wishing the same thing right now,' Bannerman replied.

She walked ahead of him to open the street door. Bannerman carried his rifle in his left hand, his saddle-bags slung across his left shoulder, and he stuck Morell's gun into his belt as he departed. He paused on the sidewalk and glanced around the street, his gaze immediately alighting on the three hardcases who had left the restaurant. They were sitting on the sidewalk in front of the general store opposite the bank, and show-ing a keen interest in the solid brick building. Bannerman regarded them for a few moments, his brown eyes filled with a chill expression, and then he went on to the jail next to the bank.

Joe Dack was seated at the desk in the law office, and Bannerman told the deputy about the hardcases. Dack nodded. 'Yeah,' he said. 'I saw them ride in yesterday, as it happened. There was a youngster rode in with them. He was sitting outside the store most of the morning and hardly took his eyes off the bank.'

'Those three are sitting in front of the store now, watching the bank,' Bannerman said. 'The youngster is in Ma Lambert's, feeding his face. He shied like a wall-eyed yearling when he walked in and saw me sitting there. It looks like we got some action coming up, Joe. Did you note the horses those guys were riding when they came into town?'

'Sure did. It's a habit of mine to watch horses.'

'Take a look along the street and see if their mounts are tied out there. They won't hit the bank unless their broncs are on hand. If the animals aren't around then drop into Ma Lambert's and run your eye over the youngster. Talk to the waitress about the weather to cover yourself.'

'Sure thing.' Dack nodded eagerly. 'Did you talk to June Tate? She was Frank's girl, you know. There was talk that they were planning to get hitched. Frank's death sure knocked her back. She ain't showing it much, but she sure is hurting over Frank's death.'

'I spoke to her.' Bannerman explained the incident with Pete Morell. 'She set me right about those three hardcases. Reckoned she heard them talking about the bank. They've got a lot of interest in a place they can't afford to use.'

'Unless they are planning to make a withdrawal with their guns,' Dack responded.

'So what about Morell? I figure him as a waster who likes to get his own way in all things.'

'That ain't far off the mark,' Dack nodded grimly. 'We've had some trouble from him, but it was mainly

49

high-spirited stuff – nothing crooked or very bad. His pa is Charles Morell, who owns the biggest cow spread in the county, and young Pete ain't had much of a guiding hand on him since his ma died just after he was born. I don't think there is any real badness in him. But watch out in case he gets his pards to try and teach you a lesson.'

Bannerman dumped his saddle-bags on the roll-top desk and looked around as Dack departed. The office was a large, square room with bare stone walls and well-scrubbed pine floorboards. There was a gun rack near the door that led into the cell block and it contained an assortment of long guns, all oiled and well polished. A pot-bellied stove occupied one corner of the room, and a long noticeboard containing an assortment of Wanted posters filled almost the whole length of one wall.

Bannerman opened the door leading into the cells and paused in the passage out back to look around the prison quarters. There were three large cages and three smaller ones. Ike Lazzard was sitting on a bunk in the nearest smaller cell. Bannerman walked along the short passage to the back door, which he checked meticulously, satisfying himself that it would fulfil its primary function. It looked to be virtually impregnable.

He ignored Lazzard and stepped back into the office to find a stocky, overweight, middle-aged man standing on the threshold by the street door. Dressed in a good blue serge suit and wearing a white Stetson, he looked ill-at-ease. His fleshy face was brooding, his pale eyes filled with uneasiness.

'You look like a man with big problems,' Bannerman observed. 'I'm Reed Bannerman, the new town marshal. What can I do for you?'

'I'm pleased to meet you, Bannerman. I'm Brent Calder, president of the First National Bank here in town. I am a mighty worried man. Some men have been watching my bank since yesterday, and I reckon they've got only one thing in mind.'

Bannerman nodded. 'I got them spotted, Mr Calder, and I'll be watching them in case they're planning to rob you. Joe Dack is checking to see if their horses are ready saddled. If they are we'll be right on their tails should they try something.'

'That's a relief to know.' Calder produced a handkerchief and mopped his face but could not stem the copious flow of nervous perspiration. 'Frank Neave said you're one of the best, and I just heard how you stopped the ore wagons entering town. But don't think Jake Moreny will let you get away with that. He can't afford to lose face around here,or he'll wind up second best.'

'Don't worry about EMC.' Bannerman permitted himself a faint smile. 'Did those three hardcases see you leave the bank?'

'No.' Calder shook his head emphatically. 'I left by the back door and went the long way around to get here. But I must be getting back. Budd Gregory, my cashier, is a good man, but I shouldn't leave him alone too long. I've got a shotgun guard standing by. John Whitney. He's dependable, and a good man in a tight spot.'

'I'm on the job,' Bannerman assured the worried banker. 'Go on back to your place and carry on as usual. I'll be pretty close to those three and if they make a move towards the bank we'll stomp them good.'

'Thanks, Marshal. It looks like you've arrived in town just in time. I'll see you later. Perhaps you'll come to supper tonight at my house.'

'I've already got an invitation.' Bannerman smiled. 'But let's get this particular crisis out of the way before making any plans for tonight.'

Calder nodded and departed quickly. Bannerman walked to the window and peered out. He could see the three men who were almost opposite, still unmoving on the sidewalk in front of the store, their attention obviously on the bank. Bannerman frowned. He could not understand why the trio were making their intentions so obvious.

He saw Joe Dack coming along the sidewalk and moved back from the window. The deputy was moving casually, but there was unmistakable haste in his stride. He came bursting into the office and looked around, trying hard to contain the excitement that was coursing through him.

'Heck, it went better than I hoped,' Dack said when he saw Bannerman. 'That youngster in Ma Lambert's went off half-cocked when he saw my badge. I stopped at his table to pass the time of day and he jumped up as if he'd been scalded. He made a play for his gun, and I only just managed to beat him to the draw. I batted him across the head with my barrel and laid him low. Heck, he almost took me unawares, spooking off like that.'

'Where is he now?' Bannerman demanded.

'I dragged him into Ma Lambert's kitchen and looked him over. He's sleeping some, but his head ain't busted. I left Billy Hodge, the old-timer who helps Ma Lambert run the cafe, covering him with a shotgun until we decide what to do with him. That bunch are surely up to no good and they look primed for trouble. So what are we gonna do?'

'Can you leave that youngster at the restaurant while we take a closer look at the other three?' Bannerman queried.

'Billy is a good man, even if he is a mite too long in the tooth these days. We better stick to the back lots until we can cross the street and enter the store from the rear. Then we can sneak up on those guys from behind.'

'That's what I'm figuring.' Bannerman drew his Colt and spun the cylinder, then returned the weapon to its holster. 'Where's the key to the gun rack? I'd like to have a twelve-gauge in my hands if the chips go down.'

Dack took a key out of the right-hand drawer of the desk and unlocked the gun rack. He selected a shotgun, picked up a box of cartridges, and motioned to Bannerman to help himself. Bannerman hefted a Greener 12-gauge shotgun in his hands and liked the feel of it. He picked up a box of cartridges, loaded the fearsome, double-barrelled weapon, and carried it open and balanced in the crook of his left hand. He stuffed spare shells into his pockets, looked into Dack's steady blue eyes, and nodded.

'We're as ready as we shall ever be,' he said. 'You lead the way round to the back of the store and we'll try to anticipate the actions of those hardcases.'

'We'll leave here by the back door,' Dack said, and they went into the cell block.

Bannerman eased his pistol in its holster as they left the rear of the jail, aware that this was where he started earning his pay …

FOUR

When they reached the back lots on the opposite side of the street, Dack rapped on the back door of the general store and it was opened instantly by a middle-aged woman wearing a big white apron over a dark dress. She stared at them, her mouth opening to ask a question, but then she registered Bannerman's badge, and stepped backwards from the door in some surprise.

'How did you know I was on my way to fetch the law?' she asked. 'There are three rough men sitting in front of the store that Otto is not easy about. He was telling me that they are bank robbers. But come in. Come in. I am afraid Otto will do something stupid if you do not stop him. He is a stickler for law and order, and was talk-ing about taking a gun to those men.'

'It's all right, Mrs Krill.' Dack eased past Bannerman and stepped into the back room of the store. 'We know about those men and we are here to check them out. This is Reed Bannerman. He's taken over the town marshal's badge from Frank Neave.'

'It was a tragedy that Frank was killed. Such a good man, he was. Have you got his killer?'

'Not yet.' Bannerman walked through to the front part of the store, stepping to the right of the doorway and gazing at the open street door, where, on the sidewalk, he could see a shoulder and part of a Stetson of one of the three hardcases seated out front. The man was lounging on a chair at the edge of the sidewalk, his attention on the bank across the street. Dack came to Bannerman's side and they eased back out of a direct line to the doorway to avoid being seen.

A big man, powerfully built, whose large head was covered by short, bristly black hair, looked round at them from behind the long counter to the right. He was wearing a spotless white apron and a white shirt. There was a cocked sixgun in his right hand. He broke into a smile when he saw them, and came towards them, holding up a finger as if warning them to remain silent.

'Joe, I am glad you could come so quickly,' he said. 'I think we got plenty bad trouble here. Did Martha tell you about those men out on the sidewalk? They do nothing but watch the bank. I think pretty soon they are going across the street to grab some money.'

'We were on our way here, Otto,' Dack said in an undertone. 'Meet Reed Bannerman. He's the lawman Frank was expecting from Kansas.'

'I am glad to know you,' Otto Krill nodded. 'It is a great pity Frank was killed before you could get here. I expect you will want to get the man who murdered him, huh?'

'You can say that again,' Bannerman said softly. 'What about those three outside? Have you heard them talking? They seem to be a mite loose-mouthed about their business. It's been reported that they've got an unlawful interest in the bank.'

'There are more than three of them,' Krill said. 'And also a youth. He was out front here all morning, watching the bank, and when he went off those three showed up. But there are three other men who have been back and forth along the sidewalk several times. They pretend not to be with the others, but they stop and talk sometimes and I know they are not strangers to one another.'

'So there are six of them!' Bannerman looked at Dack and grimaced. 'I figured there had to be more of them if they were planning to take the bank. Stay under cover in here, Joe. I'm gonna take a look along the street. Their horses are the key to this. We can expect trouble the minute they bring their nags out of the livery barn.'

He unpinned his star and repositioned it further to the left on his shirt, so that the lapel of his jacket concealed it completely. 'I'm a stranger in town so I'll be able to get away with a stroll on the sidewalk without attracting attention.'

'I'll be ready for trouble,' Dack said grimly. 'And I'll be right behind the trio outside if they make any move towards the bank.'

Bannerman put down the shotgun he was carrying and turned to leave the store by the back way. He

57

walked to the right to an alley and cat-footed along it to the street end, emerging casually to pause on the sidewalk, his keen gaze sweeping around quickly. The street was practically deserted now, with the absence of the ore wagons. He saw a stray dog walking purposefully across the street towards a rider coming slowly along it. But the animal found the effort too much in the heat, and dropped into some shade.

While Bannerman stood watching, the rider turned into the sidewalk in front of the alley between the law office and the bank and dismounted. He wrapped his reins around a tie rail and then stood rummaging in a saddle-bag tied to his cantle. To Bannerman, he looked suspicious, and when Bannerman glanced briefly at the three men seated in front of the store he discovered that one of them at least was watching him intently.

Bannerman turned away casually and looked along the street towards the livery barn. His eyes narrowed when he saw two men emerging from the barn, leading six horses between them. He began to walk in their direction, moving easily, as if he hadn't a care in the world. He came to the open doorway of a barber shop and stepped inside, his casual air vanishing the moment he was out of sight of the street.

The barber was short and fleshy, wearing a white jacket. He was snipping around the head of a cowboy seated in the chair. Looking up at Bannerman's entrance, he nodded.

'Be with you in a few moments, mister.'

'Take your time.' Bannerman drew his pistol and

checked the weapon.

The barber recoiled in fright. Bannerman jerked aside the lapel of his jacket to reveal his badge.

'Take it easy,' he said. 'I'm the new town marshal.'

'Are you after those three hardcases who have been watching the bank all day?' demanded the barber.

'Something like that. Just go on with what you're doing and I'll attend to my business.' Bannerman eased his Colt back into its holster. He saw the two men leading the horses walk by along the street, making for the general store. There seemed to be an air of nervous tension about them, and Bannerman readied himself for action.

A gunshot rang out, fracturing the silence hanging over the town. Echoes boomed sullenly before beginning to fade. Then several shots blasted. Bannerman drew his gun and stepped out to the sidewalk. He saw the three men who had been sitting in front of the store on their way across the street, drawn guns in their hands. The man who had ridden along the street was now standing in the alley mouth beside the bank, two sixguns ready in his hands. The two men with the horses were standing together in front of the store, holding reins and guns, their heads swivelling quickly as they attempted to watch the whole of the street.

Bannerman wondered what had started the shooting. He could not believe that the robbers would want gunplay before getting into the bank. He cocked his gun and moved forward to the edge of the sidewalk. One of the men holding the horses caught his movement and turned towards him, lifting a gun into the aim.

Bannerman fired instantly. The horse-holder jerked and went over backwards, dropping his gun and the reins. The three horses, spooked by the shooting, galloped off to the right, almost blundering into the three robbers crossing the street. The second horse-holder made a desperate effort to snatch at the trailing reins of the escaping horses and almost lost his grip on the animals he was holding. Joe Dack emerged from the store at that moment and shot the man in the head. Gunsmoke billowed as echoes fled across the town.

The six horses streamed away along the street. Bannerman turned his attention to the front of the bank. The three men had reached the sidewalk in front of the building, and, as they stepped up on to the sidewalk, a shotgun blasted from inside the bank entrance, sending a whirling load of buckshot through the glass in the door and tearing into the trio.

Two of the would-be robbers fell to the ground, writhing. The other staggered around and began to weave uncertainly back across the street, the gun in his hand hammering desperately as he hunted cover. Dack shot him squarely, and Bannerman engaged the robber in the opposite alley mouth. Heavy gun echoes chased across the town. Bannerman caught a glimpse of the lazing dog high-tailing it along the street, yelping in fear.

The robber in the alley mouth decided to make a run for it and hastened towards his tethered horse.

Bannerman lifted his gun and cocked it as he shouted above the dying gun echoes.

'Don't try it, mister. You'll never make it. Throw down your guns and raise your hands.'

The man did not stop, and swung a gun towards Bannerman. He was within six feet of the waiting horse when Bannerman fired, and when the bullet hit him just above the waist, his legs suddenly lost their strength and he pitched to the ground on his face and lay still as fading echoes growled away across the town

Bannerman steadied his breathing as gunsmoke assailed his nostrils. He looked around quickly, shaking his head in wonder at what had happened. He had witnessed more than a few bank robberies in his time, but these men seemed to have had no idea of how to handle the business. They had made every mistake in the book. He walked across the street to the bank. Townsfolk were appearing from everywhere, attracted by the shooting, and by the time Bannerman reached the opposite sidewalk a small crowd had already gathered, everyone calling out questions in high excitement.

The door of the bank was opened and Brent Calder appeared, accompanied by an oldish man who was clutching a double-barrelled shotgun. Joe Dack examined the two robbers who had caught the full blast of the shotgun loads, grinned delightedly at what he found, then came to stand beside Bannerman.

'I never saw anything like it.' Dack shook his head. 'Those fools did everything wrong from the start. What do you make of it, Marshal? Were they really trying to rob the bank? Heck, they started shooting before they even got inside the place. I never saw such an inexpert gang. And nearly everyone along the street knew what they were about.'

'Yet they didn't look like amateurs.' Bannerman shook his head. 'Let's get this mess cleared up quickly, huh? I'll go to the restaurant and pick up that youngster they got. Perhaps we'll learn something from him.'

'You're the boss,' Dack said, grinning.

Bannerman pushed through the gathering crowd and gained the opposite sidewalk. He walked briskly. Townsfolk were still hurrying towards the bank, all asking questions about the disturbance. Bannerman reloaded his Colt as he walked, his thoughts grim. There was a lot about the attempted bank robbery that he did not understand.

June Tate, the waitress, was standing at the door of the restaurant, looking towards the bank, her face showing the bleak turn of her thoughts. She nodded when she saw Bannerman, smiling uncertainly, and he fancied that she was relieved to see him still on his feet.

'Have you got that youngster here?' he asked.

'Billy Hodge is inside holding a gun on him. The boy hasn't got any fight in him. What happened at the bank?'

'The robbers are down in the dust.' Bannerman entered the restaurant and saw an old man standing over the youth, who was seated at a corner table, his head supported by his hands. The oldster was holding a shotgun, and looked eager to use it.

Bannerman grasped the youth by an arm and drew him to his feet. 'What's your name?' he demanded.

'I heard the shooting,' the youngster replied. `What's happened to Hack and the others?'

'Never mind about them. Just answer my questions. What's your name?'

'Toll Sweeney. I'm Hack's brother. Have you killed him?'

'He's dead, and so are the others. They made a big mistake riding into Greasewood to hit the bank. Have they tried to rob other banks?'

'Some.' The youngster nodded. 'They never had much luck though.'

'I'm not surprised.' Bannerman led the youngster to the door, and when they reached the sidewalk they were surrounded by a crowd of townsmen.

'Is he one of them robbers, Marshal?' someone demanded. 'We oughta string him up by the neck.'

'Is he one of the bunch that killed Frank Neave?' another asked.

A chorus of threats was hurled at the youngster and he cowered, covering his ears with his hands. Bannerman ordered the townsmen back, and they fell silent respectfully. He started along the sidewalk, leading Sweeney, and the youngster gave him no trouble.

When they reached the front of the jail, Bannerman paused and looked across the street towards the bank. There was an even bigger crowd there now. Men were staring at the bodies, which had been placed in a row on the sidewalk in front of the store. Otto Krill, the big storeman, was standing with Joe Dack, his beard wagging as he talked excitedly.

'Can I see my brother?' Toll Sweeney demanded, becoming animated.

'You'd better wait until he's been attended to by the undertaker,' Bannerman suggested. 'He won't be a pleasant sight right now. Let's go into the office and you can give me the lowdown on the gang's movements this past week.'

He took the youth into the office and made him sit down.

'I kept telling Hack it would be a mistake to come to Greasewood,' Toll Sweeney said, shaking his head. 'But he said the marshal was dead and we'd find it easy.'

'Tell me about the other bank raids the gang handled.' Bannerman sat on a corner of the desk. 'You said they tried to rob other banks.'

'Sure thing. Two weeks ago they held up the bank in Stanton, and that time they got a bag of money. But it didn't last long, and Hack figured there would be plenty of dough here because of the gold being mined.'

Bannerman considered the youngster. 'You didn't take an active part in robbing the bank here,' he mused. 'Were you involved in any other? Have you taken part in any unlawful activity?'

'Hack wouldn't let me do more than watch the banks. He said I was too young.'

'I'm gonna lock you in a cell until it is decided what to do with you.' Bannerman picked up the big bunch of

64

keys lying on a corner of the desk. 'Stand up.' He frisked the youngster and found no weapons on him. Sweeney gave him no trouble, and Bannerman locked him in a cell. 'I'll come back to you shortly,' he promised. 'Just think about the trouble you're in and try to come up with any information you think might help me in my job. I need to know everything about the planning of the bank raid here, and if any of your gang was in town before the previous marshal was killed.'

'I'll think about it, Marshal,' the youngster promised.

Bannerman left the office and looked around the street. Joe Dack was moving the townsfolk along now, and the undertaker and his assistant were removing the bodies of the robbers, piling them two at a time on a low handcart and trundling them along the street to the mortuary. Dack came to Bannerman's side.

'I been learning a thing or two about the gang,' the deputy said. 'Two of them have been in and out of town several times over the past week. Mebbe they knew something of Frank's killing.'

'It's possible,' Bannerman nodded. 'Frank was killed on Tuesday night, wasn't he?'

'Yeah, about nine-thirty in the evening. 'Two of the robbers were in town that night. They were drinking in Sutton's bar around that time. I got a couple of witnesses who remember seeing them. They were very quiet, not attracting any attention to themselves. It's likely they did for Frank to put him out of the way in preparation for the bank raid. Frank had a big rep in these parts, and that was probably why they killed him.'

'Was there an inquest on Frank?'

'No. But I'll talk with Doc Rennie and see if he retrieved the bullet that killed Frank.'

'And check if it can be matched up with any of the guns carried by the robbers,' Bannerman added. 'Also check the Wanted posters against the robbers. There might be something there to give us a pointer as to what's going on.'

'What are you going to do?' Dack asked.

Bannerman regarded the deputy for a moment. 'Is there anything you think I should be doing?' he countered.

Dack shook his head. 'No. I'm up a gum tree over this business; that's why I'd be no good as the town marshal. I can take orders well enough, and carry them out, but I don't have the savvy to give them. I've been in town all the time these last few weeks, but I got no idea why the mining people are acting so tough. Far as I can see there is no need for it – all these so-called troubleshooters, and local folk being threatened and frightened off. What's behind it all? And on top of that, Frank was shot in the back. I tell you, it's beyond me, and I wouldn't know where to start looking for the answers.'

Bannerman nodded. 'You're doing all right, Joe. Keep coming up with questions like those and I'll try to find the answers. Like you say, it would have been better for these mining folk to rub along with the locals instead of using roughshod tactics against them, and I'm gonna start nosing into that side of it. First off, can you tell me who is back of EMC?'

Dack looked startled, and frowned. 'Jake Moreny is boss of the outfit. But you know that already.'

'Moreny ramrods the mining operation, but he sure as hell don't own it, huh?'

Dack's face cleared and he grinned. 'You're right. Moreny is just a hardcase pushing the business along. But as for naming the men who put Moreny into the job, I couldn't say. I ain't never thought of that, and if it ever crossed my mind I guess I figured that some eastern syndicate owns it.'

'I'll have a talk with Calder. As the banker, he should know who runs EMC.' Bannerman drew his gun and checked it, spinning the cylinder before reholstering the deadly weapon. 'You get on about the business you can handle, Joe, and I'll check with you later.'

Dack nodded and Bannerman left the office to pause on the sidewalk and glance around the street. There was still a crowd of townsfolk talking excitedly about the attempted bank raid. In front of the bank itself, Brent Calder was talking with Abe Thomas, the mayor, whose keen gaze was darting around the street as if he expected more bank robbers to suddenly appear. Thomas saw Bannerman and beckoned to him.

Bannerman crossed the street, looking both ways along the thoroughfare. To his right, he could see the line of ore wagons approaching the town, but they were turning off outside of town limits and passing along the back lots to the smelter. He glanced at the people then, looking for signs of EMC trouble-shooters amongst them.

'Bannerman, Brent was giving me the lowdown on how you handled those robbers,' Thomas said. 'I sure wish I'd been here to see it. Not one of those thieves got away! That's pretty good law dealing, huh?'

'There's a lot about the way the business was handled by the robbers that don't make sense to me.' Bannerman shook his head. 'But there are more important things for me to think about right now. I was on my way over to talk to you, Mr Calder.' His dark eyes probed the banker's fleshy face. Calder was obviously elated. He seemed more animated than when Bannerman had spoken to him earlier. But then he might have been apprehensive about the presence of apparent bank robbers on the street.

'How can I help you?' Calder asked.

'I need to know who owns EMC. I figure the owners have a lot of explaining to do.'

'EMC.' Calder's expression changed instantly. His blue eyes narrowed and a wariness filtered into them. He pulled his fleshy lips into a thin line and drew a deep breath, which he held for some seconds before releasing it in a long sigh. 'I'm afraid I can't give you that information, Marshal.' He spoke in a flat tone.

Bannerman considered the banker's reaction, his pulses quickening. 'Is it secret information?'

'Not at all. I just don't know a thing about that setup.'

'As the local banker, surely they approached you in the first place to set up the business!'

'No.' Calder shook his head. 'It was all done back East, so I learned. Naturally I tried to get some of the business directed towards the town but there was nothing doing.'

'Is that what you heard, Brent?' Thomas demanded, in a surprised tone. 'Heck, I was approached by Charles Morell last year and invited to kick in with the rest of them to profit from getting the gold out of the ground. I thought everyone knew that a local syndicate had got together to run the business.'

'Charles Morell,' Bannerman repeated. 'Seems like I heard that name recently.'

'You had a run-in at Ma Lambert's with Pete Morell, Charlie's son,' Thomas said. 'Charles owns the Circle M ranch. But Pete sure ain't a chip off the old block; he's a waster.'

Bannerman's intuition started working overtime. He nodded slowly. Pete Morell had bullied June Tate, and Bannerman had already pegged him as a nasty type. He realized that Abe Thomas was regarding him closely and cut off his thoughts.

'So Charles Morell is the big wheel, huh?' he mused. 'Can you name any of the others with fingers in that particular pie?'

'Dan Ormiston, who owns Bar O.' Thomas spoke without hesitation. 'The gold strike lies squarely between their ranches. The mine practically runs along their mutual boundary. They're working together, bringing out the gold.'

'Local ranchers,' Bannerman nodded. 'But why are

69

they using hardcases to run the operation? Why were they giving the town so much grief, running their wagons along the street, jamming up the town, and threatening ordinary folks?'

'I figure those questions should be put to Morell and Ormiston themselves,' Thomas said harshly. 'And I'll be very interested in their answers. A lot of folks have complained that they are getting bad treatment from EMC.'

Bannerman grinned. 'Don't worry. I'll be asking those questions, and a lot more beside.' He looked at Calder's worried face and pigeon-holed a number of questions he wanted to ask the banker. But that was in the future, and he left the two men on the sidewalk and departed, his thoughts running fast and deep as he continued along the street.

He paused at the batwings of Sutton's saloon and peered into the building. A number of men were inside, drinking and discussing the attempted bank raid. Intending to go on about his business, Bannerman realized that he was thirsty, and pushed through the batwings and crossed to the bar. A small, bald-headed barkeep was busy pouring drinks, and he threw a glance at Bannerman as the marshal approached.

'Be right with you, Marshal,' he called.

'There ain't no need to hurry,' a harsh voice rapped, and a heavy silence followed. Men moved away from the bar with practised ease, and Bannerman found himself alone with two range-clad men who were facing him from only a few feet along the bar, their hands resting

70

on the butts of the pistols in their holsters.

Bannerman halted, his gunhand down at his side. He studied the pair and decided that they were primed for action.

'What's on your minds?' he demanded.

'Pete Morell. You gave him some bad trouble in Ma Lambert's and we aim to even up the deal. You ain't coming into this town and taking over, mister.'

'Talk's cheap.' Bannerman flexed the fingers of his right hand. 'If you've a mind to pull your guns then get to it.' His challenge set them into motion. They both reached for their weapons, and Bannerman reacted accordingly. His fingers closed around the butt of his deadly Colt, clawing it out of leather, and the weapon was cocked and ready to fire as he dropped to one knee to minimize his own target area.

FIVE

Bannerman's gun opened the shooting. The big .45 Colt bucked in his right hand, thudding against the heel of his palm as he fired. Gunsmoke flew up into his face and he held his breath against its pungent reek. His bullet took the cowboy on the right in the centre of the chest, and the man went down with his gun only half drawn. In falling, he lurched against his companion, who was bringing his gun into the aim. The man was balked, and cursed as he tried to sidestep the falling body.

Bannerman eared back his hammer and fired again, lining up his sights instinctively, aiming for the centre of the cowboy's chest. There was no time for fancy shooting. The gun blasted stridently and the man jerked as if he had run into the side of a barn. A splotch of blood appeared on his shirt front as he stiffened. His eyes rolled until only the whites were showing, and his trigger finger jerked convulsively as he died, sending a bullet into the sanded boards between his feet. He fell heavily, going over backwards and hitting the floor like a sack of flour.

Bannerman cocked his gun and looked around. The saloon had frozen into immobility. Men were staring at him, wide-eyed in shock. The bartender was agape, still pouring beer into a glass that was already filled and running over. The echoes of the shooting drummed repeatedly before fading slowly in the tense atmosphere.

Bannerman holstered his gun with a slick movement and straightened, cuffing sweat from his bronzed forehead. His ears were buzzing from the crash of the shots and he swallowed to clear them.

'Who are these men?' His voice cut through the silence that ensued. When there was no reply he continued, 'That's no more than I expected. All right, bartender, I came in for a drink. Pour me a beer.'

The tender gulped and reached for a clean glass, which he filled rapidly and set down on the bar top. He snatched up a cloth and began to mop at the puddle of beer he had spilled, his gaze never leaving Bannerman's grim features.

'I asked a question,' Bannerman rasped. 'Who are these men? They mentioned Pete Morell. Does anyone know where Pete is right now?'

The barkeep swallowed noisily. 'Them two are Billy Leat and Johnny Kinane. Leat's the one wearing the blue shirt. They are sidekicks of Pete Morell. Pete was in here earlier complaining about the way you handled him in the restaurant, and Leat and Kinane figured to teach you a lesson.'

Bannerman picked up his brimming glass of beer and held it out at arm's length. His hand was as steady as a rock. He shook his head slowly as he drank from the glass, gazing at the two men on the floor. He heard the batwings creak open and glanced over his shoulder to see Joe Dack entering at a run, gun in hand.

'What in hell is going on in here?' Dack demanded.

'It's all right, Joe,' Bannerman called. 'I've got it under control.'

Dack halted and gazed at the dead men. His lips moved silently as if he were uttering a prayer. He holstered his gun and came forward to Bannerman's side, his gaze held by the bodies, and he shook his head.

'There'll be hell to pay over this,' he said harshly. 'Where's Pete Morell? He's never far away when Leat and Kinane are around.'

'I'd like to see Pete.' Bannerman explained what had happened.

Dack shook his head. 'I should have expected something like this, knowing Pete as I do. Your run-in with him at the restaurant triggered this. Pete's like that. He can't take a beating without striking back somehow. And now he's got Leat and Kinane killed. How's Charlie Morell going to take this? He set Leat and Kinane to watch out for his precious son.'

'I got some questions I want to ask Charles Morell,' Bannerman said.

'I'll send word for him to come into town.' Dack looked around the saloon. 'Mike, get a horse from the livery barn and ride out to Circle M. Tell Morell what happened here, and warn him that Pete is in bad trouble. That'll bring him in on the run. He's bailed Pete out more times than I can count.'

The man called Mike left the saloon in a hurry, and Bannerman listened to his footsteps receding along the sidewalk.

'You better watch out for Pete now,' Dack continued. 'He's like a rattler. He'll strike when you ain't expecting it.'

'I wish he would come out of the woodwork.' Bannerman grimaced. 'You got any idea where he might be holed up?'

'He has a room at the hotel, but if he set these two up to shoot you I guess he'll have gone to ground to wait for the result. Short of searching every building in town, I reckon there's no way of flushing him out. He's got a lot of friends around here, men who collect pay from him for services rendered and women who can't resist him.'

'So it's that kind of a set-up.' Bannerman nodded. 'I get the idea.' He drained his glass and set it down on the bar top.

'Another?' demanded the barkeep, snatching up the glass. 'Everything you drink in here is on the house, Marshal.' Bannerman shook his head, his thoughts flitting swiftly over the situation. 'Thanks, but not now. I've got work to do.' He turned to the batwings, and saw a row of faces peering in over them. Dack accompanied him as he departed, and the batwings were opened for them.

'Get the undertaker to do his job with those two in there,' Bannerman said, as they strode along the sidewalk. 'I don't like this development. Pete Morell is making it a personal issue, and I'm wondering why. There's got to be more to it than the incident in the restaurant. I reckon we better check up on Pete's movements the night Frank was killed. It chokes me that Frank's killer is walking around free. We've got to do something about that.'

'Pete Morell is an angle I'd overlooked,' Dack mused. 'Pete sure is a vindictive cuss, and I know for a fact that he's got a strong hankering for June Tate, Ma Lambert's waitress. Frank stepped on Pete's toes when he fell for June. Mebbe that is why he was killed. And if that's true then it sure is a helluva note.'

They went into the law office, and Bannerman motioned to the bunch of cell keys lying on the desk.

'Let's have a few words with Lazzard,' he suggested.

Dack picked up the keys. 'I was wondering when we would get around to Ike. But I don't figure you'll have any luck with him. He's a real hardcase.'

They went through to the cells. Toll Sweeney was sitting on the bunk in his cell, unmoving and apparently lost in thought. The youngster did not look up even when Dack dragged the bunch of keys along the bars. Ike Lazzard looked up at them when they paused at the door of his cell.

'When I heard the shooting I figured you was finished, Marshal,' Lazzard grated. 'So they missed you this time, huh?' He grinned lopsidedly. 'But you won't last much longer. You'll be gone by the time the sun goes down.'

'Watch your mouth, Lazzard,' Dack snapped. 'You're in one helluva tight spot. And you figured Moreny would come in here with the rest of those buzzards you call trouble-shooters to spring you loose. Well, it hasn't happened. And it ain't gonna happen. You're in here holding the can.'

'Lazzard, you've got one chance to beat any rap that's coming to you,' Bannerman said. 'Tell me what's been going on and I'll go easy on the charges against you.'

'You've got nothing on me,' Lazzard said angrily. 'What are you trying to pull? You can't railroad me. I was only doing my job. I got a right to handle anyone who comes up against EMC.'

'You got no rights at all while you're behind bars.' Bannerman smiled. 'I'm gonna nail you for assault and causing a public disturbance. And I'll take a bet that when folks around here realize that you are finished and harmless, they'll come flocking to lay other charges against you.'

'You can go to hell!' Lazzard turned and dropped on to his bunk.

Bannerman wasted no time. He went back into the outer office and walked to the street door.

'Where are you going?' Dack called after him.

'I wanta see Jake Moreny again. He's been giving orders to Lazzard, so he's the man controlling the pressure. He should be in a cell with Lazzard.'

'I don't think you'll walk in on him a second time and get away with it,' Dack observed. 'I'd better go with you.'

'I need you around the street to watch for Pete Morell,' Bannerman told him. 'If I can't handle Moreny then I shouldn't be wearing this badge.'

He left Dack standing in the office and went out to the street. His right hand was close to the butt of his gun as he strode along the sidewalk. He saw a big man dressed in range clothes emerging from a gun store just ahead, and, recognizing him, Bannerman called out. The man halted and turned. It was Bernie Todd, the rancher who had been fighting with Ike Lazzard. A grin touched the man's battered features as he waited for Bannerman to reach him.

'You sure ain't wasting any time around here,' Todd said. 'I just heard about Leat and Kinane. But you ain't doing yourself any favours, Marshal.'

'I'll need a statement from you some time today,' Bannerman told him. 'I want to know what's been going on betweeen you and EMC.'

'I figure that will be a waste of time.' Todd shook his head. 'I'll go along with anything you say, of course. Is Lazzard still in jail? I reckoned Moreny would have sprung him by now. You should know you're banging your head against a solid wall.'

'Lazzard ain't going anywhere unless I say so. Right

now I'm on my way to pull in Moreny. Maybe you'll feel easier when I've got him behind bars. But I'm not concerned about Lazzard or Moreny; what I need is some background stuff on what's been going on. You said earlier that Lazzard was badgering you about letting EMC have the mineral rights to your range. You were fighting in the saloon with Lazzard, and I assume he pushed you into that.'

'Badgering me is putting it mildly. But I've made up my mind that I ain't gonna be pushed around any more. I'm gonna fight back. I've taken all I'm gonna swallow from that bunch of crooks.'

'That's a good idea, but don't make the mistake of trying to fight alone. Get back at them with the help of the law. Do you know who gives Moreny his orders?'

Todd looked into Bannerman's eyes, frowning as he considered the question. Then he shook his head. 'Heck, I got no idea who's back of EMC. I've always thought it would be a bunch of businessmen from back East. Ain't that so?'

'No. Charles Morell and Dan Ormiston are two of the bosses, and there may be more. I don't know. But I sure as hell mean to find out.'

'Morell, huh? Say, that could answer a lot of the questions I've been asking myself about this set-up. Charles Morell offered to buy me out months ago, and when I wouldn't sell I began to get attention from Pete and his sidekicks. There are about half-a-dozen hardcases who hang around with Pete. They are on the Circle M payroll but they sure as hell don't chase cows, and

80

they've been showing up around my place at times, making life harder than it has to be.'

'Did you report that to Frank Neave? He was a damn good lawman, and if you had complained he would have backed you up to the hilt.'

'I like to fight my own battles,' Todd admitted. 'But not any more. I'll go along with you all the way. Marshal. I'll drop by your office later and we'll talk some more.'

Bannerman nodded and went on his way. He reached the turnoff to the ore factory and entered it, striding towards the cabin where Jake Moreny had his office. The line of ore wagons coming to the factory passed behind the cabin, and a mist of fine dust blew into his face from their churning wheels. He opened the door of the cabin with his left hand, his right hand resting on the butt of his holstered gun, then paused to peer inside. There was a clerk sitting at the desk, but no sign of Jake Moreny.

The clerk looked up at Bannerman's entrance. He was a young man in shirt sleeves, his necktie loose at his throat, and he was sweating. The back door was ajar but the two windows in the building were closed, and heat had packed into the big room. 'Where's Moreny?' Bannerman demanded.

'He left about half an hour ago. Said he had business at the mine. He's always running up there on some pretext. He can't tolerate this office. I'm the only one forced to stick around here, and the heat is enough to bake my brains. If I could find another job I wouldn't think twice about taking it.'

'Do you ever see the bosses around here?' Bannerman thumbed back his Stetson and cuffed sweat from his forehead.

'Bosses?' The clerk shook his head. 'I wouldn't know them if they stepped up and bit me. They're all back East, I figure. Leastways, they would be if they had any sense. With Moreny running the place for them they don't need to be here. Moreny doesn't miss a thing, I can tell you. He's on top of the job.'

'You do the books,' Bannerman mused. 'So you know who is on the payroll and that sort of thing. What influence does Pete Morell have around here?'

'Morell? Not a damn thing! Pete wouldn't lift a finger to work. As far as I know he ain't never done a day's work in his whole life. He sure gets away with it. Apple of his pa's eye, and takes advantage of the fact. He went back East for his education, and acts like a dude when he's in these parts. I never heard of him doing anything but raise hell, and he's sure done plenty of that. Frank Neave had his hands full trying to keep Pete on the straight and narrow. You know, I never could understand Frank's attitude there. He bent over backwards to keep Pete Morell smelling like roses, even when Pete thumbed his nose at the law, like he's always doing. But nobody else in the wide world could get away with it where Frank was concerned.'

Bannerman digested the information that had come from the clerk, then turned to the door and opened it. He paused to look back at the clerk, and at that precise moment the muzzle of a gun was pressed against the nape of his neck by someone standing outside. He froze instantly, and felt a hand snake his gun out of its holster.

'That's right,' a harsh voice commented. 'Nice and easy. We don't wanta disturb the peace now, do we? You don't even have to put your hands up. But don't make the mistake of trying to resist, or you'll cross the great divide faster than a flash of lightning.'

SIX

Bannerman stood motionless under the threat of the gun muzzle pressed against his neck and was subjected to a close search. But he carried no other weapons, and a hand grasped his shoulder and spun him around. He found himself looking at two hardcases. Both were holding guns, and the black muzzles covered him steadily.

'You're a regular long-nose, ain't you?' demanded the foremost, a tall, thin man with a long face that was heavily stubbled. 'You came in here earlier and Jake didn't like it one bit when you left without getting some trouble, so he told Lew and me to watch for you coming back and give you plenty of trouble if you showed.'

'We don't have any problems about handling a man wearing a law badge,' the other said. He was short and running to fat, sweating freely, and his narrowed blue eyes carried a glint of cruelty in their pale depths. 'Let's take him out to the mine and work him over some, Hank.'

'He's outside of town limits here, ain't he?' the other demanded. 'Being the town marshal, his powers ain't worth a damn when he's out of town. Let's give it to him here in the office, but good. Jake said to beat him stupid.'

'He must be stupid already, taking on the job of town marshal,' the other observed.

Bannerman stood motionless, eyes narrowed and mind prepared for action. He had failed to check outside the shack before turning his back to it, and fancied that he was going to pay dearly for the mistake. He stood passively with his hands down at his sides, but there were leaping impulses in his mind and he waited for these hardcases to make a mistake in handling him.

'Back inside the office,' rapped Hank, grinning. 'By the time we get through you'll feel a whole lot different about holding down a law job. You ain't wanted around here, and we're gonna run you out, but good.'

Bannerman stepped back into the office, but, as he cleared the door, he whirled, his left hand reaching out to slam the door. His movement was too fast for the hardcase following him. The heavy door smashed into his face and he fell backwards with a cry of pain, spasmodically triggering his pistol. The bullet bored through the door as the shot blasted, missing Bannerman's right hip by a scant inch. Bannerman seized hold of the door and jerked it open again, moving fast.

The second hardcase had blundered into the first and they were entangled. Bannerman lunged outside.

He stepped towards the man who had stopped the door with his face and snatched at the gun that was hanging loosely in his hand. He thrust the man hard against his companion as the second man tried desperately to move clear, his gun weaving for a shot at Bannerman.

Bannerman grasped the nearest man by the throat and held him tightly, keeping him between himself and the second man. He swung the gun he had taken and whirled the butt of the weapon hard against the skull of the second man, feeling a grain of satisfaction as the impact sent a shock up his arm. The man's knees buckled, and Bannerman struck again, this time catching the man just above the left ear.

He struck a third time, aiming for the head of the man he was holding. Both men went down and lay still, and Bannerman bent to retrieve the second man's gun. He straightened, breathing hard, and shook his head as he gazed at his two prisoners. If this was the best that Moreny's men could do then his job was not going to be too difficult after all.

He glanced into the office and saw the clerk in the act of taking a rifle down from a rack on the wall behind the desk. 'Drop it,' Bannerman rapped, and the man glanced over his shoulder, then froze. 'I said drop it. Then come on out here with your hands raised.'

The clerk emerged from the office and halted to stare down at the two hardcases, who were beginning to stir. Bannerman waited patiently and, when the men had recovered their senses sufficiently, he ordered them to their feet.

'You know where the jail is,' Bannerman said. 'Let's go there now.'

'Are you arresting me?' demanded the clerk.

'You were taking that rifle down from the wall,' Bannerman nodded. 'That was a hostile act, so you're heading for the jail. The three of you can walk Indian file,' He pointed at the clerk. 'You can lead, and don't make the mistake of trying to get away: I'll shoot to kill.'

He walked behind the trio as they made their way back to the street and then on to the law office. Joe Dack was on the opposite sidewalk, and came hurrying over when he saw Bannerman.

'I knew I should have gone with you,' the deputy said: 'Did you see Moreny?'

'Not yet: I'll go for him as soon as we've locked these three in a cell.'

'At this rate Moreny won't have any men left to trouble us,' Dack observed.

They entered the law office and Dack grabbed up the cell keys: Bannerman sighed with relief when the prisoners were behind bars.

'What happens now?' Dack asked when they had returned to the front office: 'And don't leave me out of it this time. There are too many on Moreny's side for you alone to make a big impact on their numbers.'

'I figure to get Moreny soon as I can. But right now I reckon that if I can pick up Pete Morell I'll put a big damper on the trouble.'

'You saw him earlier in the restaurant, and Pete don't usually leave town so he's got to be around somewhere.

We could look in his hotel room, and I know a few places where he might be if he ain't there.'

'Let's get to it,' Bannerman decided, and they left the office.

Dack led the way to the hotel. There was a man behind the desk in the lobby, and his long face changed expression when he saw the two lawmen.

'Pete Morell,' Dack said. 'Is he in?'

The man glanced at the key board on the back wall and shook his head. 'Nope. His key is hanging there. He went out about an hour ago and I ain't seen him since.'

'We'll take a look in his room,' Bannerman said.

The man shook his head. ' I can't give you the key to any room if you ain't booked in here.'

'Then take us to Morell's room and open the door for us.' Bannerman smiled. 'But bear in mind that if Morell is inside the room he might shoot without warning.'

The man lifted the key off its hook and threw it on the desk. 'I'm doing this under protest,' he said heavily.

'I'll make a note of it.' Bannerman picked up the key. 'Where is the room?'

'On the right at the top of the stairs,' the man growled.

Bannerman led the way, and when they reached the room he handed the key to Dack. 'Unlock the door from the side nearest the lock,' he instructed. 'Then kick it open.'

Dack grinned and took the key. Bannerman drew his

six-gun and cocked it. Dack moved to the right of the door and inserted the key into the lock. He turned it silently, then stepped back a pace and raised his foot. He kicked hard and the door flew inwards. Bannerman lunged forward to cover the room, and saw at a glance that it was deserted.

Dack walked around the room, looking at the belongings that Morell had left lying around. 'He ain't the neatest cuss in the world,' he declared. He indicated a jacket lying on the unmade bed. 'Look at that, will you? Must have cost a couple of months' wages. Pete sure don't stint himself, huh?'

Bannerman nodded. He opened a wardrobe door and looked inside. It was packed with clothes. There were three store suits and several fancy shirts of the type that cowboys wear when they dress for a trip to town on a Saturday evening. A pair of expensive riding boots was in the wardrobe and Bannerman picked them up to examine them. One of them felt heavier than the other, and when he tipped it up a pistol fell out on to the bed.

'That's a strange place to keep a pistol,' Dack observed. He picked up the weapon and examined it. 'Pete carries a Remington .44. He's got small hands, and reckons a regular Colt is too heavy. But this is a Colt Pocket .41. Its barrel is only two and a half inches long. What's it doing in Pete's boot?' He sniffed the muzzle. 'It's been fired recently, and there's an empty cartridge case and four loads in the chambers.'

'A special gun for special jobs,' Bannerman mused. 'I'd sure like to know what calibre bullet killed Frank.'

'I've spoken to Ed Rennie, the doctor. He took the bullet out of Frank, and he's gonna let us have the details.'

'We need to make that a priority,' Bannerman observed. He looked at the small calibre gun closely. 'We'll both be able to identify this weapon again, huh?' he asked. 'And remember that it came out of Pete's boot.'

'You bet,' Dack nodded. 'If it was used for what I think it was then it'll put a rope around Pete's neck.'

'Let's get out of here.' Bannerman slipped the .41 into his hip pocket.

Dack closed the door and they descended the stairs to the reception desk. The hotel clerk was absent and Dack left the key on the desk. Bannerman led the way out to the sidewalk, and they both paused and looked around the street.

'Do you figure Pete has left town?' Bannerman asked.

Dack shook his head. 'Not if I know him. If he's got men out to kill you then he won't give up until it's done, or he's dead himself. Leat and Kinane wouldn't have set you up without Pete's say-so, and now they're dead I'm betting Pete is gonna follow up with another attack on you.'

'All because I laid into him in the restaurant?' Bannerman mused.

Dack nodded. 'He's used to getting his own way, and nobody has stood up to him since he was old enough to walk. He's a right wilful man these days; Frank tried many times to cut him down to size without success. Pete runs a tough bunch, and when they're out together they are unstoppable. They usually close the town on a Saturday night. The townsfolk have learned to stay clear of them.'

'And Frank let him get away with that?' Bannerman asked.

'There wasn't much Frank could do. He had a word with Charles Morell several times about Pete's behaviour, but the old man ain't got an ounce of control over his son.'

'Do you figure Pete would have killed Frank himself, or got one of his outfit to do it?'

'That's the question we've got to answer,' Dack said. 'I've been asking around, trying to find someone who saw Frank get it, but so far nobody is talking, if they know anything, that is. I don't figure anyone would have the guts to come out and accuse Pete even if they knew it was him.'

'So we've got to find Pete.' Bannerman nibbled his bottom lip. 'If he's left town then our hands are tied. Has the county sheriff been informed of Frank's death?'

'Sure thing. That's the first thing I did. But so far I ain't heard from him. There was supposed to be a deputy sheriff show up here a couple of weeks ago, but so far I ain't seen hide nor hair of him.'

'What's the sheriff like? Is he an enforcer?'

'The facts speak for themselves.' Dack shrugged. 'We're on our own here. The county ain't done a thing for us.'

'If Pete went to ground in town, where is the most likely place he'd hole up?'

'He's got a dozen places where he'd be safe. A lot of the men he hangs around with are scared of him and keep him sweet to avoid trouble. They'd hide him out and lie through their teeth for him, but not because they like him.'

'So we'll have to search the town, building by building, huh?'

'It's the only way, and we sure don't have enough men to handle that particular chore. I guess we're gonna have to wait for Pete to surface again, but in the meantime he's gonna send men out to get you. Not a good prospect, huh?'

'I'll take my chances,' Bannerman said. 'But I don't like the idea of dancing to Pete's tune.'

'If you don't want me for anything else then I'll mosey around the town and see what I can learn. Someone might open up. There are a lot of folks who don't like Pete, and one of them just might tell on him.'

'I won't hold my breath waiting,' Bannerman retorted.

Dack departed along the sidewalk and Bannerman went back to the office. As he opened the door he was called, and turned to find a tall, well-dressed man approaching from across the street.

'Marshal, I'm Ed Rennie, the doctor,' he said. 'I've got the results of my findings on Frank Neave's death. Joe Dack told me it was a matter of some urgency so I've hurried my tests. Do you have a minute to spare right now?'

'I sure do.' Bannerman held open the door for Rennie to precede him into the office, and glanced around the street before following and closing the door. He pulled up a chair beside the desk and the doctor sat down. Bannerman went behind the desk and dropped into the seat there, waiting impatiently for the doctor's report and wondering if it would pin the guilt for Frank's murder where it belonged.

SEVEN

Doctor Rennie took a folded sheet of paper from the inside pocket of his jacket and smoothed it out. His brows knitted together as he read what was written, and Bannerman forced himself to contain his impatience.

'The bullet that killed Frank?' Bannerman asked at length 'Is it a .41?' He could feel the outline of the small gun, taken from Pete Morell's riding boot, in his back pocket and pressing against his right hip.

Doctor Rennie's blue eyes narrowed as he looked up to meet Bannerman's incisive gaze. 'No, Marshal, it's smaller than a .41. Hold out your hand.' He reached into an inside pocket and took out an envelope, from which he tipped a small, misshapen slug of lead into Bannerman's palm. 'That's a .32, and I haven't come across many of them in my time. If you asked me to make an outside guess about Frank's killer, I'd say it was likely to be a woman.'

'A woman!' Bannerman drew a deep breath as a whole new vista of impressions opened up in his agile mind.

'A lot of gunmen carry a smaller pistol as a back-up weapon,' Rennie mused. 'I have it on good authority that Wild Bill Hickok favours a Smith & Wesson Pocket .32 as his hideout gun.'

Bannerman studied the slug, shaking his head. This small chunk of lead had ended Frank Neave's life.

'Frank was a good friend up in Kansas,' Bannerman mused. 'And never gave any woman a second look.'

'Here, he was walking out with June Tate and planning marriage.' Rennie shook his head. 'I'm not suggesting that she might have taken a gun to him, but I'm inclined to believe that a .32 is a woman's weapon.'

'If we found such a gun, could you tell if a particular bullet was fired from it?'

Rennie grimaced. 'Sometimes it is possible, but more often it's not safe to rely on such evidence. Have you located a .32?'

Bannerman shook his head. 'I've come across a .41, and if it had proved to be the murder weapon then a lot of my problems would be over. What else can you tell me about Frank's death?'

'He was shot from behind at very close range. The muzzle of the gun was thrust against his back between the shoulder blades. There was a scorch mark on his jacket. The bullet entered his heart, killing him instantly.'

'Frank would have been very careful around people on the street,' Bannerman mused. 'I figure his killer was well known to him, someone he trusted implicitly to have been able to get behind him with a gun.'

'That's how it strikes me.' Rennie frowned. 'No stranger could have got that close to him. Frank was a very experienced lawman.'

'Why do you think his killer might have been a woman? Not just because of the size of the gun, huh? Is there more?'

'Frank's jacket reeked of cheap perfume. It was quite strong when I got to him some ten minutes after he was shot. I checked with June Tate, and she never wears perfume. So Frank was in the company of an unknown woman just before he died, and very close to her. In contact with her, I'd say.'

'It might have been in the course of his duty,' Bannerman observed.

'But on the other hand, a woman might have led him into a gun trap.' Rennie heaved a sigh. 'I don't want to give you any false impressions, Marshal, but Frank and I used to have long discussions on just about everything under the sun. He was a well-educated man, but, apart from that, I learned a lot from him of what goes on behind the scenes in this town. You'd be surprised at all the little affairs and devious partnerships that have taken place in secret. And Frank knew about them because he was always prowling around in the night, poking into odd corners.'

'I'd like to know more.' Bannerman spoke eagerly. 'That knowledge might lead me to Frank's killer. As a matter of interest, did you manage to identify the perfume?'

'I don't think you'll get any help there. It's a kind

popular with most women in the town. I had a word
with Otto Krill, the storekeeper. His wife runs a section
in the store for women that sells all their needs. She
showed me half-a-dozen perfumes and I found the one
that was on Frank's jacket. It's a brand that most of the
saloon girls use. I doubt if you could track it down to a
particular user.'

'I'd like to take a sniff of Frank's jacket. Is it possible?'

'Sure. Drop into my office any time.' Rennie arose.

The street door opened and Joe Dack entered the
office. Bannerman watched the deputy's expression
change as he learned the facts of the bullet that had
killed Frank Neave. Dack shook his head.

'So that kills our present theory stone dead,' he said.
'Why couldn't it have been a .41? We might have
pinned the murder on Pete Morell and rid ourselves of
that particular thorn in our side.'

'Have you ever seen a .32 around town, Joe?'
Bannerman asked.

Dack shook his head. 'Nope. But we could check
with the gun shop. What Henry Ketchell doesn't know
about weapons isn't worth knowing. He might even
have sold the murder weapon to someone local.'

'Let's go and see him now.' Bannerman got to his
feet. He dropped the .32 slug into his left breast-pocket.
'I'll need this as evidence later, Doc,' he said. 'If I can
find a .32 gun and match the bullet to it then we might
have a case.'

Doctor Rennie nodded. 'We must get together soon

and have a long chat about Frank,' he suggested. 'And drop in any time to check Frank's jacket.'

'I'll do that.' Bannerman nodded. 'And I'll look forward to a chat. I need to find out what was going on around town before my arrival.'

The doctor departed, leaving his report on the desk. Bannerman explained to Dack what the doctor had said about the smell of perfume on Frank's jacket.

'Do you know if Frank was investigating anything involving a woman just before he was killed?' Bannerman asked.

Dack shook his head, his face screwed up in thought. 'I never heard him mention anything like that, and Frank would have spoken of it had there been anything. He was a man who believed in keeping me informed in case anything happened to him. But he never spoke of women, apart from mentioning last week that Pete Morell was storing up trouble for himself, chasing around after women in the town, especially those who were already involved with other men.'

'Yeah? Well that I can believe, and the sooner we can lay our hands on Pete the better. Let's go talk to the gunsmith.'

They left the office and Dack led the way along the sidewalk. The gun shop was situated between a lady's dress shop and the barber shop. Henry Ketchell, the gunsmith, was a small man who wore thick-rimmed glasses that magnified his dark eyes so that they appeared to have no pupils. His round, fleshy face remained expressionless as he listened to Bannerman's questions about a .32. Then he pointed to a glass-topped showcase.

'There's my selection of small calibre guns,' he said. 'Most of them are pocket size, with a .41 calibre, although that small gun in the top right-hand corner is a Remington Elliot .22. It's a five-shot pistol with a ring for a trigger and a curved trigger stop behind it. The only .32 I have is that Reid's "My Friend" knuckle-duster. As you can see, it has no barrel and fires directly from the cylinder. The only other .32 I've had in recent months was a Smith & Wesson Pocket .32. Not a serviceable weapon for a man. You have to be up real close to a target to hit it.'

'Have you still got it?' Bannerman demanded.

'No. I sold it some time ago.'

'Do you remember who you sold it to?'

Ketchell scratched his chin. 'I seem to remember that Brent Calder, the banker, bought it for his daughter. He said she was being pestered by a man who wouldn't take no for an answer. But I'll check my records.' He picked up a thick ledger and turned the pages swiftly. 'Here it is. Brent Calder purchased one calibre .32 Smith & Wesson some three months ago.'

'And have you ever seen another .32 around town?' Bannerman asked. 'Or sold one previously?'

'Not that I remember. There's really no call for such a small weapon. The odd gambler might carry one, but generally men prefer at least a .41 calibre as a hideout gun.'

'Thanks.' Bannerman turned to the door and Dack followed him closely.

On the sidewalk, Bannerman paused and looked at his deputy.

'I feel that I'm being sidetracked by this business of who killed Frank, but I daren't drop it in favour of getting rid of EMC's trouble-shooters, which I figure to be a greater issue. There is no trouble from the gold seekers at the moment so I'll push on with tracking down the .32 Smith & Wesson that Ketchell mentioned. You'd better stick around the street, Joe, and watch for Pete Morell. And don't take any chances if you happen to spot him.'

'I'll handle Pete with great caution,' Dack responded, and went off along the sidewalk.

Bannerman walked along to the bank, his mind filled with conjecture although he did not relax his alertness. But he could draw no conclusions from what he had learned already, and badly needed hard facts to point him in the right direction. He strode into the bank to tackle Calder, noting that repairs were already being made to the front door.

The banker was talking with Abe Thomas, the mayor, and broke off his conversation when he saw Reed Bannerman.

'Is there something I can do for you, Marshal?' Calder asked.

'I'd like a word privately,' Bannerman told him.

'Surely. Come into my office. If you would excuse us, Abe.'

Thomas nodded. 'I've got to get moving. You're doing a wonderful job, Marshal. Keep up the good work.'

'I'm just feeling my way around at the moment, Mr Mayor,' Bannerman replied with a smile.

Thomas departed, and Bannerman followed the banker into his office. Calder seemed to be on edge as he indicated a seat for Bannerman and then sat down on the edge of his chair behind the desk.

'Would you like a drink, Marshal?' he queried.

'No, thanks. I'm trying to track down everyone in town who owns a .32 pistol, and I've learned that you purchased such a weapon about three months ago.'

Calder hesitated slightly before answering, and a shadow crossed his fleshy face when his pale eyes narrowed. 'That's right,' he said. 'My daughter was having trouble from a too-ardent admirer so I bought the gun for her.'

'She must have had considerable trouble for you to buy her a gun,' Bannerman observed. 'It might have been better if you had spoken to Frank about your daughter's problems.'

'Yes, but with the type of man in this town one does not take any chances when it come to a daughter's safety.'

'I can understand that. So you bought the .32. Did you give it to your daughter?'

'Of course.' Calder held up a hand. 'Wait a moment.' His voice thinned as he continued, 'What's this all about? Why are you trying to track down a .32 pistol? And are you looking for a specific model or any .32?'

'I'm looking for the gun that killed Frank Neave. He was shot with a .32.'

'Such a small weapon? Surely a man would have used a much bigger gun.'

'Who said a man shot Frank?'

Calder froze as the implication struck him. He moistened his lips. 'Are you hinting that a woman might have done it?'

Bannerman shook his head. 'I'm merely stating facts. The rest of it is open to question. Who was the man pestering your daughter?'

'I am not inclined to talk of her affairs.'

'In that case I'll speak to her myself. Have you any idea where she is right now?'

'I wouldn't want you to bother her with such business. But I must confess that Ellen never told me the man's name.'

'But you bought her a gun in case she needed it. Did you teach her how to use the weapon?'

'She was shown how it works, and I believe she practised until she became proficient with it. After all, a .32 has a very short range. But after a couple of weeks the whole matter seemed to be forgotten. I never heard Ellen talk about the gun after that, or the man who was bothering her. I assumed that the problem had died a natural death.'

'Is there a man in your daughter's life?' Bannerman asked.

'Not that I know of.' Calder shook his head, his eyes narrowed and watchful, rather like a rabbit watching a snake.

'Well, thanks for the information.' Bannerman got to

his feet, aware that he would learn nothing more from the banker. He walked to the door of the office, and had actually opened it before Calder spoke again.

'I wouldn't like you to trouble Ellen at this time,' he said. 'The man bothering her is Bernie Todd, a local rancher. He's been making a nuisance of himself to EMC lately.'

Bannerman paused, surprised. Todd hadn't come across as that type of man. He departed, not prepared at this time to make a snap judgement. He looked around the street, undecided about what to do next, and saw Ellen Calder coming along the sidewalk. He waited for her to reach him.

The girl was tall and fair, and the sight of her again gave Bannerman the feeling that she was special to his gaze. He raised his hat as she approached, and wondered why her manner hardened the moment she saw him.

'Marshal, we meet under better circumstances this time,' she greeted, making an unsuccessful effort to make her tone pleasant. 'I don't know how you did it, but it's wonderful to have the street clear of ore wagons, just like it used to be before they found gold.'

'Those wagons won't bother the town again, Miss Calder,' he replied.

'May I expect you for supper this evening? I shall be disappointed if you can't make it.'

Bannerman edged around on the sidewalk until he was downwind of her, and caught the tang of her perfume. It smelled expensive, just as everything about her was. He did not think that the well-cut blue dress she was wearing came from Krill's store. She would have visited a big city to purchase it. As the banker's daughter, she was above average, and it showed.

'I can't promise anything at the moment,' he hedged, and saw something akin to relief show momentarily in her eyes. 'I've been plunged into the thick of the investigations that need to be made into recent events, and I shall be lucky to get off duty this evening.'

'Earlier, you promised to come,' she reproved. 'And I'm determined to hold you to that. I'm in the process of inviting a small circle of my friends to supper to meet you.'

'I don't think I'll be able to take time out from my investigations.' He spoke firmly, sensing that she was beginning to overrule his determination. 'I'm trying to piece together Frank Neave's last hours; you may be able to help me.'

'Me?' Her tone rose slightly, and Bannerman moistened his lips, aware of the fear that had for a brief moment registered itself in her eyes.

'I'm looking for the owner of a .32 pistol. I learned from the gunsmith that your father purchased one three months ago, and he's just told me he bought it for you. Do you still have the gun?'

'The .32,' she frowned. 'That was months ago! In fact, I'd forgotten all about it.'

'Do you still have the weapon?'

'Yes. I suppose so. I learned to use it, but I didn't like it, and never carried it. Anyway, the reason it was bought for me died a natural death.'

'There was a man bothering you at that time,' Bannerman persisted.

'It was nothing more than usual, and the incident wasn't serious enough for me to carry a gun.'

'Your father evidently thought otherwise. Who was the man in question?'

She looked at him for a moment, eyes narrowed, her manner suddenly closed and secretive. 'I'm not prepared to give his name,' she said finally. 'The matter was sorted out a long time ago. And it certainly had no bearing on Frank's death.'

'It might have. The gun that killed Frank was a .32. I'd like to check the weapon in your possession.' Bannerman's voice had hardened. 'What happened to it, Miss Calder?'

'I don't remember.' She shook her head. 'I believe I left it in a drawer in the dressing-table in my bedroom. I'd certainly forgotten about it. If you like, I'll go home right now, look for it and, if I find it, bring it along to your office.'

'The matter is much more urgent than that,' he replied. 'I need that gun now, and I suggest we go to your home at once and collect it.'

She gazed at him for several moments, her lips moving slightly as if she were protesting but could not give voice to the words. Then, noting his determination, she nodded.

'Very well, Marshal. If you insist then I'll do as you wish. I wouldn't want to be accused of obstructing your investigations. I was quite friendly with Frank, and I'd certainly want to do all I could to see his killer brought to justice.'

Bannerman nodded. 'We see eye to eye on that.' He fell into step with her as she turned to retrace her steps along the sidewalk. 'Who was the man who gave you trouble three months ago?'

'I can't see that anything in my life could have to do with Frank's murder,' she retorted.

'I've met Bernie Todd, and he doesn't seem to be the type who would pester a woman.'

'Todd!' She glanced at him. 'Who gave you that name?' Bannerman remained silent, and she continued along the sidewalk hurriedly, as if hoping to get away from him.

'It would help if you answered my questions truthfully and without hesitation,' he said. 'Otherwise you'll have me thinking that you're trying to keep something from me. Anything you say to me will go no further, and if it doesn't help my investigation then I'll forget about it. But I need to know what was going on in this town before Frank was killed.'

'Who mentioned Bernie Todd?' she repeated. 'Was it my father?'

'Yes. You must have given him Todd's name.'

'I did. But it wasn't Todd. I used that name to conceal the identity of the man in question.'

'Who was?' Bannerman repressed a strand of impatience when she remained silent. 'You're making a big issue out of apparently nothing,' he remonstrated. 'I don't have time for fencing around. I need straight answers to my questions, and when I check your replies, and find that they are true, then I can go on to other matters. But you're giving me the impression that you're hiding something, Miss Calder, and I won't let go until I've found out what it is.'

'I'm hiding nothing but my own business,' she responded. They reached the turn-off that gave access to the larger residences of the town, and Bannerman studied the homes of the more affluent of Greasewood's families. There were eight in all. The buildings were well spaced, separated by neat, white picket fences, and had gardens. The Calder home was larger than most, with a porch along its whole front, its woodwork, painted white, gleaming in the sunlight.

'This looks like a pleasant place in which to live,' he observed, opening the gate for her.

'I prefer city life to this.' Her manner had become less friendly, was now almost hostile, and Bannerman noted the fact. 'The men here seem to be less civilized than those in the cities.'

'That's the West for you.' He followed her to the heavy front door.

She produced a key from her purse and unlocked the door. Bannerman reached around her and opened the door, easing it wide and standing aside to permit her to precede him. They entered a long hall with stairs on the right leading up to the bedrooms. Bannerman closed the door quietly. The interior of the house was silent and still.

'If you'll wait here,' she said in a loud tone, as she crossed to the stairs, 'I'll fetch the gun for you.'

Bannerman did not reply. He remained just inside the front door, hat in hand, watching her ascend the stairs. Her friendliness had evaporated from the moment he mentioned Todd, and he was trying to work out why.

She paused at a door opening off the landing above, and glanced back down at him, her face impassive. Then she opened the door and entered the room, and Bannerman heard a man's voice begin to question her loudly, although she closed the door quickly to cut off all sounds.

Bannerman was instantly alert. There was a man in her room. He sprang into action, ascending the stairs two at a time while his right hand reached for the butt of his holstered gun. His feet made no sound on the carpeted stairs and he reached the door of the room she had entered and grasped the handle only to find that she had locked it.

With teeth clenched, he put his shoulder to the door and his lunging weight shattered the lock. The door flew inwards and he followed it, gun lifting to cover the room. Ellen Calder was standing in the centre of the bedroom, facing Pete Morell, who was in the act of reaching for his holstered gun as Bannerman confronted them.

Bannerman cocked his pistol but held his fire because the girl was between him and Morell. He could see Morell swinging his gun around the girl to shoot at him, and dived forward in a low lunge, gun uplifted. Morell's gun blasted. Gunsmoke plumed around the girl, and Bannerman felt the tug of the bullet passing through the crown of his hat.

He made contact with the girl with his left shoulder and she was sent sprawling sideways. Bannerman went down, but put out his left hand to take his weight. He saw Morell bringing his gun to bear and fancied that his own action was too slow. He supported his weight on his outstretched left hand, slewing around, using his left arm as a pivot, and kicked out with his right boot. The pointed toe caught Morell's gun arm and knocked the weapon aside. The gun exploded, and Ellen Calder cried out, her shrill tone cutting through the blasting report of the shot.

Morell cocked his gun again. Bannerman hurled himself forward, his left arm encompassing Morell's legs about knee high, jerking the man off balance. Morell fell heavily, and Bannerman's gun thudded sullenly against his head, sending him sprawling unconscious to the carpet....

EIGHT

Bannerman sprang to his feet, his gun covering Morell. He kicked the man's discarded weapon across the room. Morell was dazed, lying on his back and blinking, holding a hand to his head. Bannerman glanced at Ellen Calder and saw her motionless on the floor. She was unconscious, a patch of blood spreading on her left side on the blue fabric of her dress.

Going to her, Bannerman saw that she was losing blood fast, and holstered his gun. He ran down to the street door and jerked it open. A woman was passing the gate and he called to her.

'Fetch the doctor quickly,' he shouted, and when she turned a shocked face towards him he lifted a thumb to point at his law badge. 'Get the doctor and make it fast. Ellen Calder has been shot!'

The woman paused for a moment, then nodded mutely and set off along the street. Bannerman went back into the house, leaving the door open wide. He saw Morell on his feet, in the act of reaching for the gun he had dropped. Bannerman drew his Colt.

'Touch it and you're dead,' he rapped.

Morell paused and, still bent over the weapon on the floor, turned his head to look at Bannerman, his face grimacing with hatred and defiance. But the black eye of Bannerman's pistol gaping steadily at him made him swallow his anger and he straightened, lifting his hands shoulder high. His eyes were narrowed, calculating, weighing his chances of escape.

'Down on your face with your arms outstretched,' Bannerman rasped. 'Stay still. If the girl dies then you'll hang for killing her.'

Morell dropped to the floor and stretched his arms above his head. Bannerman holstered his gun and crossed to the inert girl. Dropping to one knee, he reached under the hem of her dress, caught hold of a petticoat and jerked it roughly, tearing most of it away from her body. He inserted a forefinger into the bullet hole in her dress and ripped the blood-soaked material, baring a wound in her left side just above the hip. He tore a strip off the petticoat, made it into a pad and pressed it against her side.

He remained hunched over the girl, holding the pad in place to assuage the bleeding, and watched the motionless Morell, who was gazing at him. Time seemed to stand still as he awaited the arrival of the doctor.

'What are you doing in this house?' he demanded.

'That ain't none of your business,' Morell grinned. 'I don't have to answer to anyone.'

'I killed two of your sidekicks a short time ago.' Bannerman wanted to shake the youngster out of his

112

arrogance, and raked his memory for names. 'Leat and Kinane. They braced me in the saloon and I had to down them.'

'You killed both of them?' Morell's face lost its smile and he started to get to his feet. Bannerman jerked his gun from its holster and covered him.

'Get back down there or I'll floor you permanent,' he warned, and Morell relaxed, but his face had paled and shock was plain in his narrowed eyes. 'You had Leat and Kinane try for me.' Bannerman could not keep anger out of his voice. 'Why? Because I'm the new town marshal or because I laid into you at the restaurant? If it was because I'm the new lawman then maybe you're the one who shot Frank Neave in the back.'

'Don't try to pin that on me.' Morell's tone was thick, his voice quivering with rage. 'I wasn't even in town when Neave got his come-uppance.'

'I'll get around to you and your doings,' Bannerman promised. He glanced towards the door when he heard footsteps entering the house, and saw Doc Rennie on the threshold, a small leather bag in his hand.

'Over here, Doc,' he called.

Rennie came to him and quickly took charge of the girl. Bannerman got to his feet and crossed to Morell.

'On your feet,' he rapped, covering the man with his gun. 'Give me half a chance to shoot you and I'll take it.'

Morell arose and stood with his hands raised shoulder high. There was a sneer on his lips, and Bannerman was tempted to erase the expression with his fist but

113

resisted the urge. A thought struck him and he walked to the dressing-table by the bed. Events had made him forget that he had come to this house to collect the .32 gun Ellen Calder owned.

Keeping an eye on the watchful Morell, Bannerman searched the drawers in the dressing-table, and his eyes narrowed when he failed to locate the .32. He looked at the motionless figure of the girl. Rennie was busy examining her.

'Can you manage here, Doctor?' he asked. 'I need to jug Morell.'

'I'll need help shortly to get Ellen to my place,' Rennie said.

'What are her chances?' Morell demanded. 'I didn't shoot her deliberately. My gun went off when he hit me.'

'She's hurt bad.' Rennie grimaced. 'But it's too early to make a judgement on her condition.'

'I'll send help to you,' Bannerman promised. He decided to come back later and make a thorough search for the missing gun. 'On your way, Morell,' he directed. 'Head for the jail.'

Morell walked to the door, his shoulders swinging, and Bannerman poked him between the shoulders with the muzzle of his gun. Morell swung around, hands reaching for Bannerman, who stepped backwards half a pace and threw a shrewd left hook which connected with Morell's jaw. He staggered, tripped over the doorstep, and landed heavily on the path.

Bannerman heard the gate click and looked up

swiftly to see Joe Dack approaching fast, gun in hand.

'I heard shots,' Dack said tensely, 'and was worried about you. What's going on?'

'Ellen Calder stopped a bullet. Go in and help the doc, then come back to the office.' Bannerman reached down and secured a grip on Morell's collar. He shook the inert man roughly and Morell groaned and opened his eyes. Bannerman hauled him to his feet, maintaining his grip, and thrust his prisoner towards the gate. 'Let's get on to the jail,' he rapped. 'You can sleep all you want when I've locked you in. And don't try anything else; you're wasting your time trying to better me.'

When they reached the door of the bank, Reed Bannerman thrust Morell inside. Brent Calder was behind the counter talking to his teller, and came forward quickly when he saw Bannerman's drawn gun. Bannerman explained about Ellen Calder and the banker's face turned grey with shock.

'I'll come back to you later,' Bannerman promised, as he took Morell out of the bank.

Calder did not reply. He hurried past Bannerman and went running along the sidewalk towards his home.

By the time Bannerman reached the door of the law office there was a crowd of townsfolk at his heels, all chattering about the arrest of Pete Morell. Bannerman ushered him into the office and closed the door on the crowd. He took his prisoner through to the cell block and locked him in a cell. Morell stood at the door of the cage and rattled it furiously.

'Wait until my pa hears about this,' he grated. 'He'll

show up with twenty men, and you'll be in bad trouble.'

Bannerman ignored the threat and went back to the office just as Joe Dack opened the door and stuck his head inside.

'Grab your gun and come quick,' the deputy said urgently. 'We got big trouble coming.'

Bannerman drew his gun and checked it, reloading the spent chambers without comment. When he walked out to the sidewalk he saw a party of tough-looking cowpokes reining up in front of the office. Two big men were in the forefront of the group. One was dressed in a store suit and a white Stetson. His horse was a big black stallion that stood uneasily with rolling eyes, its jaw working spasmodically, dropping flecks of foam into the dust. The other man was range dressed, big and square-looking, with hard-bitten features and cold, watchful eyes.

'Charles Morell of Circle M and Sam Bickford, the ranch foreman, with some of the Circle M outfit,' Joe Dack informed Bannerman, planting his feet on the dusty boards of the sidewalk. He rested the thumb of his right hand along the top edge of his cartridge belt, his fingers close to the butt of his gun.

Bannerman looked into Morell senior's impassive face and was unable to read anything of the man's intentions. Townsfolk were pushing back from the front of the office, a tense silence settling over them. Bannerman's gaze flitted around the grouped riders, noting the odds. There were five cowboys backing the foremost two riders.

'You got business with me?' he asked, genially.

Charles Morell stirred in his saddle. 'You've pulled in my boy for shooting Ellen Calder.' His harsh voice boomed out of his barrel-like chest.

'Ellen Calder was shot, and I'm holding Pete for the shooting,' Bannerman confirmed.

'You got any witnesses to say Pete did it?' Sam Bickford, the ranch foreman, spoke out of the left side of his mouth, his voice rasping like an old file. His right hand rested on the butt of his holstered gun and he looked ready to draw it.

'I'm the only witness,' Bannerman replied. 'If you want to know more about the incident then come into the office.'

All the riders stepped down from their saddles as Charles Morell dismounted, and they followed their boss like sheep as he moved on to the sidewalk.

'Send your crew someplace else,' Bannerman said. 'They don't come into the office.'

Morell gazed into Bannerman's harsh face for what seemed an eternity. Bannerman remained impassive, but his eyes were glinting. Morell turned to Bickford.

'Take the boys to Sutton's saloon for a drink, Sam,' he said. 'Don't let 'em get out of hand. I'll yell if I want you.'

The big ranch foreman looked as if he would argue, but he nodded bleakly and turned away, chivvying the cowpokes to the nearest saloon. Morell moved towards the door of the law office and Bannerman stepped aside for him. He met Dack's enquiring gaze and grinned fleetingly. They entered the office and Dack closed the door against the townsfolk who came surging forward.

Bannerman told Morell what had led up to the shooting of Ellen Calder, and the rancher remained silent, not surprised by what his son was supposed to have done.

'I want to see Pete,' he said. 'Why is he behind bars? He didn't shoot the Calder girl deliberately. I figure you're as much to blame for her getting hurt by swiping Pete with your gun. Why are you picking on my boy? Sure, he's a bit wild, but he ain't bad.'

'I figure I might have made a mistake about him,' Bannerman observed grimly. 'I'm beginning to think I should have shot him while I was at it. He's some hellion, Morell. He got his two pards, Leat and Kinane, to brace me, and they're both dead. That's the main reason why he's behind bars.'

'You're new around here.' Morell's harsh gaze was unblinking as he turned to the watchful deputy. 'Dack, mebbe you better give our new town marshal a run-down on who is who in this county. You know the Morells don't answer to the law.'

'If that's the way things have been handled around here in the past then you've got a surprise coming,' Bannerman said. 'I'm in the law saddle now and I'll run things by the book, without fear or favour. If you don't like that then stay out of town.'

'Talk's cheap.' Morell's eyes glinted. 'How'd you figure to make that stick against the cowmen on the range? I got them all in the palm of my hand. They'll jump in on my side with both feet if I crack the whip.'

'In that case I'll hold you responsible for any trouble I get around here.' Bannerman kept his tone quiet. 'You'll be the man I pick up and charge for any violation of the law.'

Morell shrugged. 'Let me see my son,' he rasped.

Bannerman picked up the bunch of keys and led the way into the cell block. He stood by while Charles Morell went to the door of Pete's cell. Ike Lazzard got up from the bunk in his cell and came to the door. He sneered at Bannerman as he gripped the bars and shook them.

'Hey, Boss, get me out of here,' he rasped. 'I got work to do.'

Charles Morell ignored the trouble-shooter, and Bannerman smiled.

'It looks like you ain't having much luck today, Lazzard,' he observed. 'Mebbe I'll turn you loose later so you can get yourself into more trouble.'

'You ain't got nothing against me,' Lazzard snarled.

'You got to get me outa here, Pa,' Pete said to his father. 'I didn't shoot the girl deliberately.'

'I'm not holding you for shooting Ellen Calder,' Bannerman said. 'You're behind bars because I had to kill the two sidekicks you set on me. That's a serious charge, and I'm gonna make it stick.'

'You ain't got no proof of that,' Pete retorted. 'Just because they was pards of mine. I didn't see them at all today. They'd been drinking heavily for two days, and what happened was a joke that went too far. They was gonna give you a hard time, that's all. They figured to welcome you to Greasewood, and you gunned them down.'

'I'll talk to John Beech,' Charles Morell said. 'He's a good lawyer, Pete, and he'll have you out of here in no time.' He turned to leave but halted when Bannerman barred his way. 'Are you figuring to give me trouble?' he demanded. 'You're on dangerous ground as it is. I only got to snap my fingers and you're dead.'

'I need to ask you some questions.' Bannerman led the way back into the office.

Dack took the bunch of keys from Bannerman and locked the door to the cell block. Morell walked to the desk and stood beside it, his face showing impatience.

'What's on your mind?' he demanded.

'I understand that you're one of the bosses of EMC,' Bannerman said. 'So explain to me why your trouble-shooters have been giving this town so much grief.'

Morell shook his head. 'I don't know what you mean. I don't have any say in the running of the mining business.'

'Jake Moreny is running the operation for you, and he had the ore wagons moving along main street until I stopped them. What way is that to run a business? And your so-called trouble shooters have been riding roughshod over the townsfolk. I'd like to know why such tactics were used.'

'I don't know about that.' Morell moved towards the street door, his heavy features impassive. 'Talk to

120

Moreny about it. The only time I would interfere in the business is if the schedules were not maintained. So far, Moreny has done everything right, and that is fine by me. He's got my backing.'

'Sure,' Bannerman smiled. 'But Moreny's actions today are not all right by me so you'd better start looking for another mining expert. Moreny is gonna see the inside of a cell the minute I can get around to him.'

Morell did not reply, and Bannerman made no attempt to stop the rancher when he opened the door to depart.

'Remember that I'm holding you responsible for the actions of every man working for you,' Bannerman called, as the rancher left the office. 'Anyone gets out of line after this and you answer for it.'

'Heck, you laid down the law to him,' Dack observed, when Morell had departed. 'But how do we make it stick?'

'We sure as hell don't sit around waiting for his next move,' Bannerman responded. 'Let's get out there and pick up all the trouble-shooters you can identify. Then we'll go for Moreny himself. With the hardcases behind bars most of the trouble will be over.'

'I hope you know what you're doing.' Dack looked doubtful. 'I got the feeling that everything is gonna suddenly blow up in our faces.'

'Are there any men around town that the law can call upon for help in an emergency?'

'A few regulars are always available for posse work and the like.' Dack grimaced. 'But they wouldn't be any

121

use as deputies in the kind of shoot-out we've got coming up here.'

'You think it will end in shooting?' Bannerman studied the deputy's expressionless face and, when Dack nodded slowly, he asked, 'Do you have any problems with that?'

'Nope. It's an accepted part of the job. I think you're going about it the right way. The more of Moreny's men we can pull in now, the less we'll have to face when the chips are down.'

'And if we can get Moreny himself then there won't be a lot of fight left in the hardcases,' Bannerman mused.

'Now you're talking.' Dack grinned and drew his pistol to check the loads and the action of the weapon.

Bannerman stepped out to the sidewalk and looked around. There was still a group of townsfolk, standing nearby, hoping for more action. Dack emerged from the office and went to an oldish man, spoke to him, and the man nodded.

Dack turned to Bannerman. 'This is Tom Billings,' he said. 'He works as town jailer when we need him, and I figure we want someone in the office now we have prisoners in the cells.'

'Fine,' Bannerman nodded. 'Don't open any of the cells while we're away, Billings. Keep the street door locked and don't open to anyone but Joe or me.'

'I know how to handle the job,' Billings replied. 'I'll keep a loaded shotgun close to hand, and you better sing out before you try to come into the office.'

Bannerman nodded, and Dack handed the jail keys to the jailer, who entered the office and locked the door.

'Let's get on with it,' Bannerman observed. 'We'll make a round of the town. Point out any trouble shooters you recognize, and we'll jail them.'

'Let's check out the saloons first,' Dack said. 'There's about ten that I know of and they're usually hanging around main street, ready for trouble.'

They went to Sutton's saloon and pushed through the batwing doors. Bannerman wondered if they had made their first mistake for Morell's cowhands were inside, lined up at the bar and drinking silently. All eyes swivelled to look at the entrance at the sound of the batwings creaking open.

'Over there,' Dack said in an undertone. 'At that corner table. They're trouble-shooters.'

Bannerman glanced across the room and saw three men playing cards at the corner table. They looked uneasy when observing the two lawman heading their way. Bannerman stopped by the table, his hand close to the butt of his gun.

'Hands on the table and keep 'em there,' he said easily, drawing his pistol, and the trio froze when the gaping muzzle covered them. Bannerman smiled, his eyes glinting. 'Take their guns, Joe.'

'What's going on?' demanded one of the men in a blustering tone. 'We ain't broken the law.'

'You work for EMC.' Dack moved around the table to disarm them.

'And we're providing free lodging for EMC hands,' Bannerman announced. He waited until Dack had finished. 'Now let's go quietly to the jail.'

'You won't get away with this,' one of the others snarled. 'Wait till Moreny hears about it.'

'We're on our way to tell him,' Bannerman smiled. 'And when we catch up with him he'll get the same invitation we're giving you. Now get up and start moving.'

The trio arose from the table, two of them overturning their chairs in the process. They were reluctant to obey, but with Bannerman's steady gun covering them they had no choice and headed for the batwings. But when they reached the spot where Sam Bickford was leaning on the bar, the foremost trouble-shooter looked at the big ranch foreman and spoke quickly.

'Hey, Bickford, we work for Morell. Are you gonna let these two jail us? Morell won't be pleased if you stand by and let it happen.'

Bickford straightened from the bar, his right hand dropping to his gun butt. The rest of the cowpokes stiffened.

'Stay out of this,' Bannerman rasped, his gaze on Bickford. 'This is law work. Stick your nose in and I'll arrest you.'

'I take my orders from Morrell,' Bickford said out of the corner of his mouth. 'If he tells me to come for you, then, mister, I'll do it. There's no two ways about that. Where is Morell? Is he still in your office?'

'No.' Bannerman motioned to Dack to move the prisoners on, and the deputy dug the muzzle of his pistol into the foremost man's belly and urged him through the batwings. The others followed. Dack stayed close to them, but Bannerman remained in the saloon, matching Bickford's harsh gaze. Bickford shrugged and turned back to the bar and Bannerman left the saloon.

'Well that was easy,' Dack observed, when the three were safely behind bars. 'But you can bet it'll get tougher after this. Those Circle M hands will pass on the word that we're rounding up EMC trouble shooters, and the rest will be ready for us.'

'We're going after Moreny now.' Bannerman opened the street door, stepped outside, and waited for Dack to join him.

The deputy paused in the doorway of the office, his hand dropping to his gun butt. The sound of hoofs suddenly sounded loud in the silence hanging over the town, and Bannerman braced himself when he saw half-a-dozen riders spilling quickly out of an alley opposite to spread out into a single line facing the law office. He spotted Jake Moreny leading them. All were heavily armed, and looked intent on raising hell.

The waiting townsfolk evidently gained the same impression as Bannerman for they faded away quickly, running into doorways and alleys, dropping into any kind of cover and leaving the street in front of the law office deserted and still.

Moreny spoke to his riders and they came forward in a line, knee to knee, moving slowly, crossing the street towards the spot where Bannerman and Dack were waiting.

Bannerman straightened his shoulders and eased his right hand nearer to the butt of his gun. It looked as if a showdown had arrived.

NINE

'It's good of you to drop by, Moreny,' Bannerman called. 'I was about to look for you. Get off that horse and come into the office. We got some talking to do.'

'No talk.' Moreny eased his bulk in the saddle. 'We've done talking. You got some of my men behind bars and I want them out. I don't pay Ike Lazzard to sit around in jail.'

As he spoke, the mining engineer reached for the gun on his hip, and the men with him used his movement as a signal. But a harsh voice shouted from Bannerman's left and all movement ceased. Moreny looked towards the source of the interruption, and Bannerman threw a quick glance to his left and saw Charles Morell standing on the sidewalk with Sam Bickford beside him and their five cowhands backing him.

'What's going on?' Morell demanded.

'We got some trouble-shooting to do.' Moreny was gripping the butt of his holstered gun. 'That's what you pay for so let us get it done.'

'I never paid you to fight the law of the town,' Morell rasped. 'I don't see how that could benefit EMC. Back off, Moreny. Pull in your horns.'

'Get out of here and leave me to do my job.' Moreny returned his gaze to Bannerman, still ready to fight.

'Make up your mind,' Bannerman rasped. 'I got business to attend to. Pull your gun, or get down and come with me.'

'They got Pete behind bars,' Moreny snarled at Morell. 'Are you gonna let them get away with that?'

Morell rapped an order to his cowpokes and they drew their weapons and covered Moreny's crew. Bannerman wondered at this change of attitude from the rancher, and waited to see how the situation would develop.

'I told you to back off,' Morell said. 'Keep pushing and you'll be out of a job.'

'What makes you think I'll want to continue if you interfere with my decisions?' Moreny hunched his shoulders, and Bannerman, watching the man closely, figured that he was trying to push himself into disobeying his employer. ' I need my men out of jail, and if you ain't gonna back me up in this then you can go to hell. I'll quit cold.'

'Hank Carter is your assistant.' Morell's voice was harsh, unforgiving. 'Hand over to him and get out. As of this minute you're through, so move out.'

Bannerman did not relax. He was wondering what had gone on behind the scenes between these two hard men, and could not help thinking that perhaps it was

Gun Peril

some kind of a set-up for his benefit. He was surprised
when Moreny accepted the discharge at face value. The
mining engineer spoke to his men and backed his
mount a few paces, then whirled the animal and started
away along the street. Bannerman fought an impulse to
call him back. He turned to face Morell as the rancher
came forward, followed by his men. Sam Bickford, the
ramrod, remained at the rancher's shoulder, looking
impassive but resolute, apparently ready to back up his
boss whatever happened. Bannerman figured that he
had merely changed one set of adversaries for another.

'I've been looking into Moreny's handling of his job
and I don't like what I've discovered,' Morell said
harshly. 'He wasn't following my instructions when he
started in on the town. Now he's finished, and I'll talk
to the man who will take over his job. There'll be no
more bad behaviour, and they won't interfere with the
townsfolk. Any of my employees who steps out of line
will be discharged instantly.'

'That's a step in the right direction,' Bannerman
observed. 'But it doesn't explain why Moreny acted as
he did in the first place. Murder has been committed,
and I'm gonna find those responsible and make them
answer to the law.'

'Sure, and if you need help then Bickford and these
men will help you with the job. You hear that, Sam? Stay
in town and be ready to back the law.'

'What about Pete?' Bickford demanded

'I'm confident the marshal will get to the bottom of
Pete' s trouble and release him in due course. Whatever

happens, we don't go against the law. But we will be around to see that the law is handled properly. And don't forget that you and the men are on duty even if you are staying in town, so keep out of the saloon.'

Morell turned and walked off along the sidewalk. Bickford gazed at Bannerman for some moments, then holstered his gun, and the men backing him did likewise. Bickford shrugged, then grinned.

'You heard the boss,' he said. 'Nobody better step out of line or there'll be hell to pay. We're here to back up the law.' He looked squarely at Bannerman. 'Just say the word and we'll go along with you.'

'All you've got to do is stay out of my way,' Bannerman said grimly. 'I don't need your help.' He glanced at the motionless Dack, who was standing just behind him. 'Joe, stay in the office and wait for my return. There are one or two loose ends I need to tie up.'

Dack nodded and turned to the door of the office. Bannerman went along the sidewalk, passing Bickford and his men. He saw Charles Morell ahead, now talking to Brent Calder in front of the bank, and when he reached the two men he paused and addressed the banker.

'How is your daughter, Mr Calder?'

'Doc Rennie says she'll be all right in a few weeks.' Calder glanced at the expressionless Morell then returned his gaze to Bannerman. 'She was conscious when I saw her, and said the shooting was not deliberate. You hit Pete Morell with your gun barrel. Pete's gun

130

went off as he fell, and it just happened to be pointing in Ellen's direction.'

'I know what happened,' Bannerman said. 'And I'll go into the circumstances when I can get around to it. What I want to know is why Pete was alone in your house at that time. You were here at the bank and your daughter was on the street.' He explained the sequence of events. 'So why was Pete waiting in your house?' he ended. 'Was he using the place as a hideout to keep away from me? And why did he pull his gun when I confronted him? He sure didn't act like a law-abiding citizen.'

'You burst into that bedroom,' Charles Morell said. 'Pete might have thought you were a thief who had broken into the house. I reckon I would have done exactly the same as him if I'd been in his boots. There's been much lawlessness around here, and everyone is hair-triggered to respond to it.'

'From what I've heard, much of the lawlessness came from Pete and his sidekicks.' Bannerman shrugged. 'It won't hurt Pete to stay in jail while I make some enquiries. Where is the doctor's office?'

'A block down on the other side of the street,' Calder told him.

Bannerman crossed the street and walked along the opposite sidewalk, his thoughts moving fast. He felt that he was missing something significant in this set-up, perhaps a vital fact that had escaped his notice from the beginning, and until he dug it out he could not hope to solve the mystery of Frank Neave's death. But at the moment he had nothing tangible to work on.

He arrived at the door of the doctor's office and entered to find Rennie sitting at a desk inside a large room. The doctor got to his feet when he saw Bannerman.

'How is Ellen Calder now, Doc?' Bannerman asked.

'Her life is not in danger, but she's badly hurt and it'll be weeks before she's back on her feet. I guess you've come to look at Frank's jacket.' Rennie went to a cupboard and took out a light-blue jacket which he held up, revealing the rear of the garment, and Bannerman saw a small bullet hole high up in the back. There were scorch marks on the fabric. 'Frank's jacket,' he continued in a harsh tone, holding it out to Bannerman. 'Smell the perfume on it.'

Bannerman put his nose close to the jacket and sniffed. The reek of cheap perfume on it was powerful, and he frowned. 'Heck, that's strong,' he observed. 'It smells as if Frank was doused in the stuff, and I thought, by what you said earlier, that he had been in a woman's company just before he died. But he didn't pick up that smell by making normal contact with a woman. She must have poured it over him.'

Rennie nodded. 'And I'm afraid that it isn't a pointer to Frank's killer,' he said. 'It was little enough in the way of evidence anyway. I've been asking questions around town, trying to piece together Frank's last movements, and I learned only a few minutes ago that when Frank was in a saloon about an hour before he was shot there was a bust-up between two saloon girls. Frank stopped them and they went into their dressing-room, where the trouble flared up again. It seems that Frank stepped in once more and was accidentally hit by a bottle of perfume thrown by one girl at another. The stopper came out of the bottle and Frank was drenched with perfume. It raised a big laugh in the saloon at the time.'

Bannerman nodded. 'It looks like we're up against a brick wall in this investigation,' he observed.

'I learned a little more from June Tate, the waitress at Ma Lambert's restaurant. She told me Frank was edgy when he dropped into the restaurant for his supper an hour before he was killed. He seemed to have something on his mind. But talk to her and see what you can make of her statement.'

'I'll do that. Is Ellen Calder conscious? I need to talk to her. I want to know why Pete was in her home, apparently hiding from the law.'

'She was sleeping when I left her some minutes ago.' Rennie got to his feet. 'I'll take a look at her, but I don't think she'll be able to answer questions for a couple of days at least.'

'All right, I'll leave her for now. I might get some answers from Pete himself, although I doubt if he could tell the truth even if he wanted to. Keep me informed of Ellen's progress, Doc.'

Bannerman departed and paused on the sidewalk. He looked around, his keen eyes missing nothing of his surroundings, and shook his head as he went on to the restaurant. But June Tate was not there. She had just gone off duty, and Ma Lambert, a short, greatly overweight lady in her fifties, directed him to the small shack where the waitress was living.

Bannerman walked to the edge of town, where a collection of small buildings housed the less important inhabitants of the town. There was a row of shacks fronting the creek, with the EMC smelter on the far side. The monotonous sound of ore being crushed and processed was ceaseless, and too loud to live with, Bannerman decided as he paused at the third shack in line, a rickety, unpainted little building, and knocked on the flimsy door.

He fancied that he heard a sound from inside the shack as he waited, but the noise from the smelter baffled his ears. He tried the door, and when it opened easily at his touch, a gun crashed inside the shack. He ducked as a bullet bored through the woodwork, crackling ominously in his left ear and barely missing him.

He drew his gun as he lunged forward in a low dive into the shack. His shoulder crashed against the door, sending it flying open. He hit the dirt floor heavily and rolled as the gun inside the shack hammered again, and this time he felt the stinging pain of a bullet burn on the outside of his upper left arm. He caught a vivid impression of June Tate sitting in a corner with a man standing by her, swinging the gun in his hand in an effort to line up on Bannerman's fast moving figure.

Bannerman was already thrusting his gun up into the aim, and he fired quickly, sending two slugs at the man. He rolled out of the doorway and got up on one knee, gun ready to fire again. But the man was falling to the floor, his pistol slipping out of his suddenly nerveless grasp, and there was a splotch of blood showing on his pale-blue shirt.

June Tate stood up, shaking in fright, hands to her mouth, blue eyes betraying great fear. Bannerman pushed himself up, covering the fallen man, but saw at a glance that the danger was over. He lowered his gun, blinking against the sting of burned powder. His ears were ringing from the noise of the shots.

'What was going on here?' he demanded.

June tried to speak but her voice was choked with shock. She swallowed and drew a deep breath, her breathing rasping with gun fumes. Bannerman led her out of the shack. When he let go of her she staggered, and he grasped her firmly.

'I'm sorry,' she gasped. 'That man in there is Ben Delmont, one of Pete Morell's bunch. He was waiting for me when I got home from the restaurant, and threatened to kill me for telling you about Frank's death. I told him I hadn't said anything to anyone, but he didn't believe me.'

'So what do you know about Frank's death that you haven't told me?' Bannerman's voice was insistent.

She shook her head despairingly. 'I was helping Frank in his work. He suspected that someone was planning to steal gold from EMC while it was in the bank awaiting shipment to the East. I heard small talk in the restaurant that was close to being illegal, and passed it on to Frank. But somehow Pete found out what I was doing and forced me to keep him informed of Frank's activities. He

threatened to have Frank killed if I didn't go along with
him. At first Morell only put pressure on me, but then he
started showing an interest in me, and I became really
frightened. He threatened that if I didn't do what he
wanted then Frank would die. I daren't tell Frank
because he would have gone after Pete, who always had
half-a-dozen tough guys around him. Finally, Pete told
me to tell Frank that some bank robbers had been
brought in to steal the gold in the bank and that I'd overheard Pete saying he was going to meet them in the alley
beside the livery barn. Frank went there, and was shot in
the back by Ellen Calder. Since Frank's death I haven't
known what to do. Morell had threatened to kill me if I
didn't keep quiet, and, when all the robbers were killed
this afternoon, Delmont turned up here accusing me of
warning you about them. I'd be dead now if you hadn't
shown up when you did.'

'Ellen Calder killed Frank?' Bannerman set his teeth
into his upper lip as some of the facts of Frank's killing
slipped into place in his mind. So that was why a .32
pistol had been used.

'That's what Pete told me.' June was trembling, her
face ashen. She clutched at Bannerman's arm. 'I didn't
dream that they were planning to kill Frank that night.
and I was only trying to help him with his job. That's
why I told you about those robbers before they went to
the bank. I wanted you to get even for the law.'

'But Charles Morell is one of the owners of EMC,'
Bannerman mused. 'Is Pete so low that he'd rob his
own father?'

'He's worse than that. He's been getting at some of the wives of the prominent men in town, and even Ellen Calder was eating out of his hand. She shot Frank because Pete told her to. That's the kind of influence he had over her.'

Bannerman sighed as he considered. 'Let's get back to the night Frank was killed,' he said. 'Did Morell say exactly what happened?'

'No. But he gloated over it, hating Frank as he did. He hadn't dared use one of his men to kill Frank because it could have been traced back to him, so he made Ellen do it. He threatened to kill her father if she didn't.'

'I can't believe that girl would do such a thing.' Bannerman shook his head in disbelief.

'Pete hinted that he had other things against Ellen which he used to pressure her into it.'

'What could she have done that was so bad?'

'You'll have to ask her about that.'

'Bannerman, are you all right?' Joe Dack stepped into view from around the corner of the shack. He was holding his pistol, but holstered the weapon when he saw no danger. 'I heard the shooting and figured someone had got you.'

Bannerman explained what had occurred. Dack looked into the shack and emerged again shaking his head. 'Delmont was a real hardcase,' he said. 'I'm glad you've put him where he belongs. But Ellen Calder deliberately shooting Frank in the back takes some swallowing. Are you sure about that, June?'

'That's what Pete told me.' The girl suppressed a shudder, and Bannerman grasped her shoulder and steadied her.

'We'll go along to the office and get some of this down in writing,' he decided. 'Then we'll talk to Pete and see what he has to say. And we'd better question Toll Sweeney and find out what he can tell us about the bank robbery. His brother was running that gang of robbers, and he must have heard them talking over their plan to hit the bank. If we put some pressure on him he might open up and tell what he knows.'

They left the shack and made their way back to the law office, Dack rapped on the locked door and called for Tom Billings to open up but there was no reply. The deputy moved to the front window and peered into the office.

'Hey, Tom is lying hogtied on the floor,' he announced, 'and the door to the cells is wide open.'

Bannerman cursed under his breath and hurled himself at the door of the office. It shook under his assault but did not yield. Dack joined him and they kicked the obdurate woodwork until it gave way. Bannerman lunged into the office. Billings was moving jerkily on the floor, trying to get free of his bonds. A kerchief had been pushed into his mouth to gag him and Bannerman removed it while Dack ran into the cells.

'It was Bickford and the Circle M riders,' Billings gasped. 'Joe said Morell told them to stand by for the law so I thought it was all right to let them into the

138

office when they asked to come in. But when I opened the door they grabbed me. They took Pete out of his cell and left by the back door.'

Dack emerged from the cell block, shaking his head. 'The place is empty,' he said disgustedly, 'They took Toll Sweeney with them and all the others. The back door is standing wide open.'

'How long ago did this happen?' Bannerman asked.

'Five minutes, I reckon.' Billings rubbed the back of his skull. 'They must have had their horses ready out back because I heard them ride away immediately.'

'And they took Toll Sweeney with them,' Reed Bannerman glanced at Dack. 'Joe, take a turn around the town and see if you can locate Pete It's just possible that he didn't leave. I want to question June a little more and get her statement down on paper. If you see any of Morell's men around then just watch them until I catch up with you shortly.'

Dack departed. He had barely closed the street door when shots hammered, and he came lunging back into the office.

'A couple of men across the street,' he said, as he drew his gun. 'I didn't get time for much of a look at them, but I recognized a couple of those cowpokes who were backing Charles Morell.'

'So they're coming out into the open.' Bannerman moved to the front window to peer out and a bullet shattered the glass, causing him to duck. He drew his gun and went to the door. When he opened it he drew more shots, and crouched in the doorway, peering out.

He saw gunsmoke drifting from the alley mouth almost opposite, and caught a glimpse of movement there. Triggering his gun, he sent two well-placed shots into the spot, and a man lurched into view, fell forward on to his face and lay unmoving.

A spate of shots blasted out the silence and a fusillade of bullets smashed into the front of the office, shattering the rest of the window and thumping into the back wall, gouging and splintering the woodwork. Dack thrust the muzzle of his pistol through the window and began shooting rapidly, and Bannerman joined in when he saw four men coming at a run across the street, firing as they closed in.

His steady gun knocked over one of the attackers and the others turned and dived back into cover. Dack put one of them down before they disappeared, and then the shooting ceased.

'I reckon that will discourage them.' Dack reloaded his spent chambers and spun the cylinder. 'What say we go out now and I take over, before Morell can bring in more of his men?'

Bannerman pushed himself to his feet, his gun already reloaded and ready for further action. He stepped out to the sidewalk, darting quick glances around the deserted street. A man stepped out of the alley opposite, lifting a gun into the aim, and Billings fired a shotgun from the office window, the heavy charge of buckshot flailing into the man, who pitched over backwards and lay crumpled on the sidewalk.

Gun echoes were drifting away across the town as

Bannerman crossed the sidewalk and stepped down into the street, gun ready in his hand. Dack emerged from the office and stood on the sidewalk, covering Bannerman.

'Joe, you better get around town and call out the men who usually help the law in an emergency. It looks like being round-up time now, and if we're gonna beat the odds then we have to strike before Morell can gather his gunhands.'

'Some of our gun help are coming already,' Dack replied, and Bannerman saw movement further along the street. 'Don't shoot them. That man with the rifle is Seth Roan, the blacksmith. And just behind him, toting a shotgun, is Otto Krill from the store. Otto is a regular fire-eater. Abe Thomas is across the street, heading this way, and there's John Whitney, the bank guard, coming up fast. Frank arranged for a small bunch of reliable men to come running any time there was trouble.'

Bannerman nodded, watching the street as the townsmen came up and Dack explained what had happened.

'I saw Pete going into the hotel about ten minutes ago,' Abe Thomas said. 'I thought you'd turned him loose. He usually gets away with anything he does. I didn't know he'd been busted out of jail or I'd have gone after him.'

Doc Rennie suddenly appeared on the opposite sidewalk and came unsteadily towards the law office. Bannerman frowned as he watched the medico's approach, for Rennie had blood on his face and shirt-front. The man staggered, lost his balance and sprawled on the sidewalk. Bannerman started running towards him, and Rennie was trying to get to his feet when the marshal reached him.

'What happened to you, Doc?' Bannerman grasped the man's arm and helped him to his feet. The doctor arose, but was unable to maintain his balance, and Bannerman supported him as he reeled like a drunk. There was a large bruise on the doctor's forehead and blood had seeped from a gash just above his hair-line and was dripping on to his shirt.

'Pete Morrell just paid me a visit,' Rennie gasped. 'He hit me with his gun, and while I was trying to recover, he went into Ellen Calder's room and shot her dead.'

Bannerman caught his breath, aghast at the news. Pete must have realized that he had reached the end of his rope and was determined to kill off everyone who could testify against him.

TEN

Bannerman helped the doctor into the office and arranged for Dack to remain with Billings to take care of June Tate and Rennie. Abe Thomas departed to enlist the help of more townsmen, and Bannerman went along the street to the bank. He found Calder in his office, and informed the man of his daughter's death. The banker was shocked. He collapsed into his seat behind the desk, his face ashen and sweat beading his forehead. Bannerman, fearing Calder was suffering a seizure, went to the man's side and unfastened his collar. He poured a slug of whiskey into a glass and held it to the banker's lips.

Calder drank the whiskey and, by degrees, the colour returned to his face. But his eyes were filled with deep shock. He looked up at Bannerman, shaking his head as he tried to come to terms with the grim news.

'It's my fault,' he gasped. 'None of this would have happened if I had done the right thing in the first place. But I let the Morells dictate to me and had no

143

option but to go in with Charles when he started his mining enterprise. Then Pete started his own particular brand of business and I was forced to go along with him against his father. But Pete turned out to be as crooked as a snake and involved me in his bad deals. By that time I was in his power, and he played it for all he was worth. He even threatened to kill Ellen if I didn't keep in line, and that girl was all I had.'

Bannerman listened intently, taking in the facts. The banker was badly shocked by Ellen's death and hardly knew what he was saying. But Calder poured himself another whiskey, drank it greedily, and then jerked open the drawer of his desk. He picked up a pistol and checked it.

'What are you planning to do?' Bannerman asked.

'I'll put Pete where he belongs; something I should have done when he first latched on to me.' Calder got to his feet, swaying like a drunk.

Bannerman snatched the gun out of the banker's hand and pushed the man back into his seat. 'Just stay out of it,' he said grimly. 'Leave the law-dealing to me. So you've been in cahoots with Pete Morell huh? Is there anything else you can tell me that will help me put an end to the trouble around here?'

Calder shook his head. His determination seemed to run out of him like water dripping from a hole in a bucket. He leaned forward and supported his head in his hands, his elbows on the desk. Bannerman gazed at him for a moment, then departed. He needed to arrest Pete Morell.

When he reached the sidewalk, Bannerman was faintly surprised to see that the evening was now well advanced. Shadows were creeping into the dusty corners of the town. The sun was well over into the western part of the sky, which was raked by golden streaks of rapidly fading glory. Over in the east, the brilliant blue of the heavens was assuming a deeper grey, and turning even darker towards the horizon, where the blackness of approaching night was slowly usurping the brightness of the long day.

With his thoughts teeming, Bannerman continued along the street, checking the buildings for Pete Morell. He entered the hotel to learn that Morell had not been seen, and encountered the same situation wherever he enquired. Finally he reached the stable, and entered into near darkness. The glimmer of a lamp in the small office attracted him and he went to it, finding the stableman slumped on the seat behind a dusty desk which had a pool of congealing blood on its top. The man's throat had been cut and he was dead.

A noise sounded from inside the gloomy stalls, and Bannerman drew his gun as he leaned over the lamp and extinguished it. He heard a horse stamp, but that was not what had alerted him. He moved to one side of the doorway and peered out into near impenetrable darkness. The keen smells of the building caught his nostrils. He strained his ears for unnatural sound, then slipped out of the office and put his back to the inside of the front wall, his gun ready for action.

At that moment, footsteps sounded outside the open

doorway. Bannerman cocked his gun. He drew a deep breath to steady himself and crouched a little, minimizing his target area. An indistinct figure stepped into the doorway.

'Hold it right there,' Bannerman called. 'Keep your hands clear of your body. I'm the town marshal. Who are you?'

The newcomer halted. 'What's this, a hold-up?' he demanded. 'Don't bother, if it is. I ain't got a red cent on me.'

'I told you I'm the law. Who are you?' Bannerman's right index finger was tense against the trigger of his .45. His eyes were slitted to make out details of the man's figure, which was in silhouette.

'Tom Jenson. I ride for Bernie Todd. I came into town to warn the boss that Circle M riders have moved in across our line. Four of them are camped at our water-hole, and they look like they intend to stay. I can't find Todd in town and I'm on my way back to the ranch.'

'Todd was here earlier. I broke up a fight he was having with Ike Lazzard. Light a lantern and take a look around the stable. See if Todd's horse is here.'

Jenson struck a match and turned to a lantern suspended from a post just inside the doorway. He gazed curiously at Bannerman when yellow light filled the interior of the barn.

'Check the horses,' Bannerman said, his gun uplifted as he looked around the barn.

Jenson obeyed, and Bannerman watched him

intently. The man made a round of the stalls before coming back to him shaking his head.

'No sign of Todd's horse,' he said. 'I better head back to the ranch. Is it all right if I saddle up?'

'Go ahead. Is Pete Morell's horse in here?'

'Morell never puts his mount in here. There's a stable back of Moreny's cabin over by the smelter. That's where Pete's horse will be if he's in town.'

'Thanks.' Bannerman moved to the doorway and departed. He placed his back to the wall of the stable and looked around, checking for trouble. The town was quiet; too quiet, he decided, and kept his gun in his hand as he crossed the street and made for Jake Moreny's cabin near the smelter.

There was a light shining in the window of the mining-engineer's cabin, and Bannerman moved stealthily in a half-circle to approach the building from the side. He made a circuit of the cabin, and saw a stable positioned behind it. The stable was in total darkness and he turned to the cabin.

There were no trouble-shooters around when he approached the rear of the cabin. He paused in its shadow, ears strained for unnatural sound, then moved to the front corner and rounded it to peer through the dusty window beside the door. He cocked his gun when he saw Jake Moreny inside, busily stuffing papers into a small leather case. Ike Lazzard was sitting at the desk, drinking whiskey from a bottle.

Bannerman moved to the door and kicked it open. Moreny froze in shock. Lazzard sprang to his feet, reaching for his gun, and Bannerman shot him in the centre of the chest. Lazzard sprawled across the desk, blood seeping on to the papers strewn there. Bannerman stepped inside the cabin, his gun levelled. He closed the door with his left heel and confronted the shocked mining engineer.

'You're about ready to hightail it,' Bannerman observed.

'I've had my fill of this place.' Moreny relaxed a little, his hands down at his sides. He was wearing a holstered six-gun but made no attempt to touch the weapon. Bannerman waggled his levelled Colt.

'Get rid of your gunbelt and then we'll talk,' he said.

Moreny unbuckled the belt and let it drop to the floor. 'Like I said earlier,' he said easily, 'there's nothing to talk about. You heard Morell fire me. I'm getting out. I've done nothing that's been against the law; I'm not the kind of fool Lazzard was.'

'It won't be as easy as that,' Bannerman shook his head. 'The law wants you.'

'I've got nothing to answer for. All I did was my job.'

'Why did you insist on bringing the ore wagons through the town? And why all the aggravation?'

Moreny shrugged. 'I was merely obeying orders, and while I did what I was told I was allowed to get on with the job. If I had stepped out of line I would have suffered like everyone else around here.'

'Pete Morell?' Bannerman did not relax his alertness.

Moreny regarded him for a moment, shaking his head. Then he moistened his lips. 'So you've been

148

learning things about the set-up, huh? I'll do a deal with you, Marshal: I'll tell you exactly what has been going on and you let me split the breeze out of here.'

'No deals. Frank Neave was murdered, and I want everyone who was in on that.'

'Pete is responsible for every crime ever committed around here. Either he planned them or caused them to happen. He brought the bank robbers in. He had Neave killed. It was his idea to run the ore wagons along the street and block the town while the bank was being robbed. But you showed up and put a stop to that and the raid failed.'

'Where is Pete now?' Bannerman asked.

Moreny shrugged. 'You've got him in jail.'

'Sam Bickford and the Circle M cowpokes got him out.'

'The hell you say! Charles Morell won't like that.'

'I think he gave Bickford the order to do it.'

'Well you think wrong. Charles is interested in his gold mine, and that's all. He's given up on Pete. For years he's turned a blind eye to Pete's shenanigans, putting the curb on only when Pete went too far. But since he formed EMC, Charles has been too busy to watch his son, and Pete has got out of hand. He's gone too far now to be helped or stopped, and it wouldn't surprise me if Bickford took Pete out of town and killed him. Bickford would do anything for Charles Morell. I reckon he would stick his hand in a branding fire if Charles told him to.'

Bannerman remained silent, not wishing to cut off the flow of information. But Moreny clamped his jaw shut and shook his head. He gazed at Bannerman for a moment, trying to gauge his chances of escaping retribution. Then he sighed.

'I know where Pete will be holed up while his pards kill you, Marshal, and I'll give you that information in return for the chance to walk free out of here.'

Bannerman waggled his gun. 'Spill the beans and I'll consider letting you go,' he said. 'I can't do any better than that.'

Moreny shrugged as he considered. Then he drew a deep breath. 'My bet is that Pete has taken over Calder's house. He'll be waiting for the banker to get home to take the bank keys off him, then steal EMC gold from the bank before hitting the trail for other parts. Check Calder's house, and if Pete ain't there then he'll be at the back door of the bank with a wagon. The bank raid should be going ahead now darkness is here. That business with the bank robbers this afternoon was staged to throw the town off guard. A bank raid was foiled and no one would expect another raid so quickly.'

Bannerman motioned to the door. 'You can go with me,' he said. 'If you've told the truth then I'll release you as soon as I clap eyes on Pete.'

Moreny looked as if he would argue, but closed and locked his case and carried it as he walked to the door. He paused in the doorway and peered out into the night. Bannerman moved forward to follow, and glimpsed the ragged gunflash that flared redly in the impenetrable gloom surrounding the cabin. Moreny uttered a cry and spun around, the case falling from his hand. He lurched against the door post, then fell heavily.

Bannerman swung his gun and sent a shot into the lamp, plunging the cabin into darkness. He crouched over Jake Moreny and felt for a heart beat. Moreny was dead. Curbing his impatience, he awaited developments. A burst of rapid shooting erupted outside, fired by at least three guns that sprayed the cabin with crackling, thudding slugs. Bannerman flattened himself on the floor, covered by Moreny's body, which was hit several more times in that lethal outburst. He refrained from returning fire, remaining silent and deadly as he awaited the next move.

Remembering the lay-out of the cabin, he crawled to the back door and arose to open it, freezing when it creaked. But there was no response from his assailants, and he wondered if the men out there were aware of his presence in the cabin. It was possible that they had come just to kill Moreny.

He peered into the darkness, listening intently, his gun poised for action. Nothing stirred outside, and he crouched and ran from the cabin, making for the black mass of the stable. He gained its shelter and paused, standing erect, his back to the wall, checking for trouble. The night breeze blew into his face and he canted his head slightly to listen for unnatural sound. There was nothing. It seemed that the attackers had withdrawn.

He moved around the stable and used it as cover, walking away from the area and heading for the street.

He found an alley and moved along it, feeling his way through the darkness. The town was silent, as if it were holding its breath, and when he gained the sidewalk and looked around he was surprised to see that most of the buildings around him were in darkness. Even the saloons seemed to be closed, and there were no men on the street. He saw that the law office was in darkness, and so was the bank. He crossed the street, staying off the boardwalk, his feet making no sound in the rutted dust. Turning into an alley on the further side, he walked its length to the back lots and paused to look around. Here, as on the street, nothing stirred, and there was deathly silence.

But presently he heard a horse stamp somewhere ahead and close by. He narrowed his eyes, trying to pierce the darkness, and as his sight became accustomed to the night he slowly made out the details of a wagon and two horses standing at the rear door of the bank. He walked forward slowly, and saw a figure emerging from the rear door of the bank. There was a muffled thud as a heavy item was loaded on the wagon.

Bannerman flattened himself against a wall and waited. The single figure re-entered the bank and two men emerged, carrying a long box between them. They had difficulty lifting it up to the wagon bed. Reed Bannerman waited for them to re-enter the bank then closed in.

When a single figure came out of the doorway carrying two bulging sacks, Bannerman struck shrewdly with the barrel of his pistol. The man gasped and fell in a sprawling heap. Bannerman dragged him aside, searched him, removed a pistol from his holster, then waited for the others. Moments later two men reappeared with another box.

'Put down the box and raise your hands,' Reed Bannerman grated, and the two men obeyed immediately. 'I can see you perfectly well,' he continued, 'so don't try anything or I'll kill you. Where is Pete Morell? Is he in the bank?'

'Pete?' gasped one of the men. 'This has got nothing to do with Pete. We're working for Charles. This is his gold from the mine and we're moving it to a safe place because of the attempted raid here this afternoon.'

'Who's handling this job? Is Calder inside the bank?'

'No. Calder wouldn't let Charles have the gold. He figured it was too dangerous to move it.'

'So you're stealing it.'

'Not exactly. You better go talk to Charles Morell about it.'

'Where will I find him?'

'At the Cattleman's Hotel.'

'How many of you are here?'

'Three. Say, where's Art?'

'He's sleeping over there. One at a time, get rid of your guns. Do it slow or you'll draw a slug apiece.'

The men disarmed themselves and raised their hands again.

'There'll be hell to pay over this,' one of them said.

'You can say that again,' Bannerman responded. He looked into the wagon and saw that several boxes and a

153

number of canvas bags had been loaded. 'Take them back inside the bank. Don't make the mistake of trying to best me. It'll only get you killed.'

The men obeyed reluctantly, and Bannerman watched them intently. By the time they had finished the chore the third man was stirring, and Bannerman dragged him to his feet and pushed him towards his pards.

'Carry him to the jail,' he directed. 'I'll be at your backs all the time, and I've got a nervous trigger-finger so don't try anything.'

'You won't get away with this,' snarled one of the men.

'Let me worry about that,' Bannerman retorted.

He herded his three prisoners through the night to the rear of the jail, and they traversed the alley to the street to arrive at the front door of the office. Billings opened the heavy door in response to Bannerman's call, and Joe Dack stood just behind the jailer with a levelled shotgun in his hands. There was worry on the deputy's face, which cleared at the sight of Bannerman.

'What's happening around here?' Bannerman demanded. 'The place looks like a ghost town.'

'Abe Thomas has warned folks to lie low. I heard some shooting, and figured you'd been caught out.'

Bannerman explained what had happened and the prisoners were locked in the cells.

'What happens now?' Dack demanded.

'I want to talk to Charles Morell then pick up Pete. If I can handle it right then the trouble will die here and now. Failure will mean an out-and-out shooting war.'

'Knowing Pete as I do, I reckon you'll have to kill him to stop him. He won't give up, and if he has been breaking the law like we figure, then death is the only outcome. But you better not go out there alone again. You'll need my gun to back you.'

'I can handle the office,' Billings said. 'Take Joe with you, Marshal. He ain't doing no good sitting around here drinking my coffee.'

'To the Cattleman's Hotel then,' Bannerman said.

'What will you do about Bickford and those cowboys if we bump into them? They'll certainly be around guarding Morell.'

'We'll cross that river when we come to it,' Bannerman responded.

Billings let them out of the office and they paused until the door had been bolted behind them. Bannerman checked his gun as they walked along the street. As they reached the entrance to the hotel, where a solitary lantern on a post cast dim yellow light across the sidewalk, three men moved out of the darkness beyond the entrance and went into the building.

'Sam Bickford and two of those CM cowpokes,' Dack said.

Bannerman drew his gun as he stepped on to the sidewalk. He moved ahead of Dack and crossed the threshold of the hotel, stepping into the lobby, his gun lifting to cover the three men at the reception desk.

'Throw 'em up,' he rapped.

Bickford came spinning around as if he had swallowed greased lightning. He made a play for his gun and the two men with him followed his action. Bannerman thumbed back his hammer and fired as Bickford's pistol cleared leather. Gun thunder blared as his bullet took the ranch foreman in the chest. The impact knocked the big man backwards off his feet. Bickford fell across the desk and rolled to the floor.

Dack opened fire on the two cowpokes as they bought into the grim play. He downed one of them, and then he and Bannerman fired simultaneously at the second man, dusting him both sides with their heavy slugs. Gunsmoke drifted across the lobby.

The hotel clerk was standing behind his desk, frozen by his nearness to death, his face chalky white.

'Where's Charles Morell?' Bannerman demanded.

The clerk pointed up the stairs, unable to speak.

'I know which room he's in.' Dack headed for the stairs as he reloaded his pistol.

Bannerman was content to follow, thumbing fresh shells into his gun as he ascended the stairs. He glanced down at the lobby to check his back and froze in midstride when he saw movement at the street door. Four men were entering from the sidewalk, and one of them was Pete.

'Joe,' Bannerman called urgently, and the deputy swung around.

Pete Morell lifted his gun from its holster, his teeth bared in defiance. Aware that the chips were down, he was filled with determination to fight to the death. Bannerman cocked his gun as he lifted the weapon to cover the newcomers. His ears were singing from the shock of the previous shooting and drifting gunsmoke was irritating his nostrils.

The crashing detonation of shots was overwhelming in the close atmosphere of the building. Bannerman clenched his teeth as his thumb released the hammer, and his first slug took one of the cowpokes in the throat. He had aimed at Pete who ducked behind his human shield, and, as Dack joined in the shooting, Pete turned and dashed out of the hotel.

Bannerman triggered his smoking gun. The remaining cowboys dropped out of the fight, and Bannerman dashed down the stairs. But, as he ran towards the street door in grim pursuit, Morell backed into the entrance, the gun in his hand down at his side. Bannerman was surprised to see Charles Morell appearing in the entrance, a levelled Colt in his hand covering Pete.

'You've gone too far this time, Pete,' the cowman rapped. 'You were stealing my gold from the bank! Robbing your own father! And you schemed with half my crew to work against me. I've a good mind to hand you over to the law.'

Bannerman reached Pete's side and snatched the pistol from the man's hand. Charles caught a glimpse of the grim scene in the lobby and froze in shock. Bannerman threw Pete's gun across the lobby.

'The law is handling this,' he said sharply.

Charles Morell lowered his gun, his face showing conflicting emotions. 'What are the charges against my son?' he demanded.

'Among other things, Pete murdered Ellen Calder in the Doc's house,' Bannerman said implacably. 'We'll surely hang him for that.'

Charles Morell was visibly shocked by the news. 'There was a time when I thought it was just high spirits with you, Pete,' he said, shaking his head. 'But you're bad right through to the middle. I'm glad your mother never lived to see this day.'

'Don't let them hang me, Pa.' Pete lifted his hands, palms upward. 'Don't let them take me.'

Charles Morell gazed at his son with disgust showing plainly on his weathered face. Then he sighed heavily and brought his gun up into the aim, pointing the muzzle at Bannerman. 'Blood is thicker than water,' he said sorrowfully, thumbing back his hammer. 'And I always supported the law until you stepped out of line, Pete.'

His voice was drowned out by the crash of Joe Dack's gun, and a splotch of blood appeared on the rancher's shirt over his heart. He fell back against a doorpost, spun away and dropped to the floor. Pete cursed and spun towards Bannerman, his right hand reaching into the side pocket of his jacket. Bannerman fired as Pete brought a small pistol into view, and his bullet took Pete in the right shoulder, causing the .32 he was holding to fall from his suddenly nerveless gunhand. Bannerman slammed his gun barrel against Pete's skull, and the youngster collapsed with a groan.

Joe Dack came forward and picked up the .32. He held it out to Bannerman. 'You've been looking for one of these,' he said. 'I reckon Pete has got a lot of explaining to do, huh?'

Bannerman took the gun and examined it, assuming that it was the weapon that had killed Frank Neave. He slipped it into a pocket, needing it as evidence. The gunsmoke drifting inside the hotel lobby was irritating his throat and he stepped out to the sidewalk, gulping the night air blowing along the street.

He stood quietly for long moments, thinking of the events that had taken place since his arrival a few short hours before. It came to him then that the problems existing when he rode in had all been solved with gunfire. There were still details to be checked, but by and large it was over. He saw lanterns being lit along the street as the town came back to life, and was aware of relief in his chest as Dack hustled a dazed Pete Morell out of the hotel and escorted him along the sidewalk towards the jail.

He suddenly felt tired, sickened by the blood-letting and the killing. But he knew someone had to do it, and had accepted long ago that he was one of the chosen....